The Casebook of

Inspector Armstrong

Volume I

Martin Daley

The Irregular Special Press
for Baker Street Studios Ltd
Endeavour House
170 Woodland Road
Sawston
Cambridge CB22 3DX

First Published 2011
This edition © Baker Street Studios Ltd, 2011
Text © Martin Daley, 2011

ISBN: 1 901091 51 1 (10 digit)
ISBN: 978 1 901091 51 9 (13 digit)

Cover design: Martin Daley & Antony J. Richards

Front cover picture courtesy of Old Photos

Armstrong image courtesy of Janet Wainwright

Typeset in 8/11/20pt Palatino

For two little Bannisters

Contents

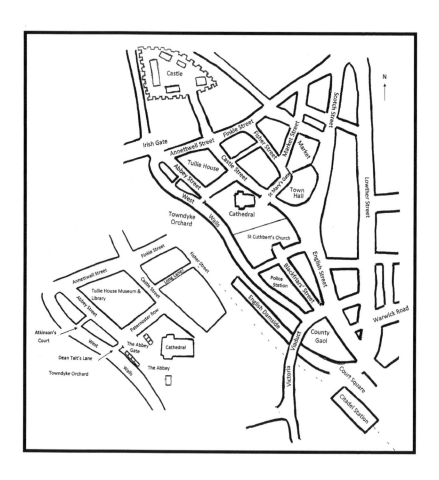

Chapter One

The Morgue

Having undergone its postmortem the previous afternoon, the body of Salvatore Rucci lay on the porcelain autopsy table under a plain white sheet in the morgue at the Cumberland Infirmary in Carlisle. All was silent; the stark, functional room was painted throughout with a drab monotonous whitewash, broken only by the odd set of exposed pipes. The low ceiling, stone floor and white porcelain sink combined to created a stillness that turned a dripping tap into a loud, echoing gloop.

In the corridor outside, footsteps that produced a similar resonance could be heard approaching. The noisy fiddling of a clanging set of keys was followed by the rattling of the doorknob and two men entered – one in a medical gown, one in a light brown knee-length overcoat and carrying his bowler hat.

Picking up a file and – out of sheer habit – lifting the first page with the tips of his fingers, Doctor James Bell gave his companion an appraisal of his findings.

"The murder weapon was thrust into the victim's neck from the front with a vicious upward motion. This has been done with such ferocity that the knife has actually protruded through the back of the neck, puncturing the thyroid cartilage and the larynx along the way, as well as shattering the top of the spinal column and therefore severing the brainstem. For good measure, upon the withdrawal of the weapon, it has been twisted in order to sever the right carotid artery – hence the copious amounts of blood at the scene. The victim would have been dead within seconds – if not from the original injury, he would have bled to death very quickly. The perpetrator knew exactly what he was doing, Inspector. This man Rucci hasn't just been murdered, he has been executed."

Detective Inspector Cornelius Armstrong was casting his eye around the room: he noticed the dried bloodstains splattered on the floor – presumably as a result of many a gory autopsy; against the wall, next to the sink, was a tall glass fronted cabinet that contained a wide range of surgical instruments; beside it was a short bench on which stood half a dozen specimen jars. The policeman was still coming to terms with the almost overwhelming stench of the mortuary and its icy coolness, when the doctor's words snapped him back into reality. He gave a long look at the medical man knowing that this was an extraordinary case by Carlisle's standards; murders were the stuff of London legend, not our sleepy backwater – and atrocities such as this were virtually unheard of.

Doctor Bell drew back the sheet covering the body. Armstrong looked down at the corpse; it was almost unrecognisable from the individual he had seen less than four days earlier. The jet-black hair was neatly slicked back, while the indistinguishable lips and face had turned into a bluish inert membrane. There was a horizontal black gash about three inches long running from the middle of the cadaver's neck towards its right ear.

The policeman stood transfixed, conscious of the appalling injury juxtaposed with the skill of the pathologist who had otherwise prepared the body for burial without any other outward signs of desecration. Armstrong was a man with over fifteen years experience and one who considered himself worldly wise, but he knew the enormity and brutality of this case would thrust the small local force and him in particular into the local – perhaps even national – spotlight. An article had already appeared in the *Carlisle Journal* the previous day suggesting that officers from Scotland Yard – with greater experience of such cases – might be brought in to investigate.

Fortunately, Chief Constable Henry Baker considered Inspector Armstrong his best man and had no hesitation in supporting him in his investigation, whilst stressing to his subordinate the need for quick results given the high profile nature of the case. The fact that the murder had taken place within yards of the Police Station inflicted further pressure on Baker to have the case solved quickly; and Armstrong himself was taking the criticism personally as not only was the crime committed within a stone's throw of his place of work, but it was within a similar distance from his own lodgings on Abbey Street.

Within forty-eight hours of the murder, Armstrong had bought himself and his boss some time by piecing together the sequence of events that took Rucci to the corner of Dean Tait's Lane and West Walls on the night of Saturday 7th November 1903. Moreover, he was confident he knew the killer's movements immediately before and after the crime; but worryingly, the murderer remained at large and no motive for the crime had been forthcoming.

Doctor Bell produced a large brown envelope, "I've put the file together as you requested, Inspector – photographs of the postmortem and a copy of my findings." He gave them to the policeman.

"Thank you, Doctor," said Armstrong. Having completed a high profile case involving a theft from the castle only weeks earlier, the detective had been looking forward to returning to the mundane existence of the small town policeman. *Some chance of that*, he thought as he left the pathologist; he knew he had much to ponder.

Chapter Two

A Rude Awakening

Four days earlier, Cornelius Armstrong could never have imagined the sequence of events that brought him to this point. He had completed his uneventful day around six o'clock and strolled the short distance along West Walls and through Atkinson's Court to his lodgings at 22a Abbey Street – a journey of little more than five minutes normally, but the policeman was feeling decidedly under the weather and the five minute stroll became more of a ten minute traipse.

His lodgings were a suite of rooms on the first floor of the town house owned by Mrs. Isabella Wheeler, whose husband ran his cycle shop immediately next door. The Wheelers and their daughter Emma occupied the ground floor and basement. Cornelius climbed the five steps to the front door and selected one of the keys from a large ring; trudging up the stairs and along the landing, he discovered Mrs. Wheeler in his sitting room having just delivered his evening meal.

"I've just lit the fire, Mr. Armstrong, and it's steak and kidney pudding tonight," she said pointing to the large silver dome on the table.

"Thank you Mrs. Wheeler, you're an angel."

His housekeeper left, and Armstrong looked around his little sanctuary and smiled – content to be away from the people and bustle experienced by the policeman – his books; his piano; the roaring fire.

After devouring another of Mrs. Wheeler's finest, he poured himself a glass of rum and sank into his favourite green, leather-bound rocking chair by the fire. General drowsiness led to a state of ruminative abstraction. The detective held up his glass to the light; through the distortion of the crystal glass, he looked at the book-lined wall of his sitting room. The entire room seemed to expand and contract in synchrony with his thumping heart. He threw his head back and poured the liquid down his throat, wincing at the sharpness of the alcohol.

"Early night, I think," he told his empty glass.

Within minutes, Armstrong was sleeping deeply, and inside the portal to his subconscious his dreams swirled almost uncontrollably throughout; noises and images blurred as, gradually, an intermittent high pitched sound rose above all others and appeared to be willing Cornelius awake. The distant, mysterious echo progressively dragged him towards consciousness, until he woke with a start at a commotion downstairs. Bolt upright in his bed, he tried to come to terms with what was happening; the cause of the disturbance was a persistent banging on the front door of his lodgings.

Armstrong quickly grabbed his dressing gown, lit a paraffin lamp and hurried down the stairs. As he reached the bottom he saw Mrs. Wheeler had beaten him to it; he also saw a police constable on the other side of the threshold.

Joe Brady had initially tried to be as discreet as anyone can be whilst insistently rapping on the door-knocker to wake the occupants inside at such an unsociable hour. After several seconds of realising the futility of his actions, he resorted to banging on the door with the side of his fist. Finally, the bleary-eyed lady of the house opened the door.

"I'm sorry to disturb you, Mrs. Wheeler but can I see Inspec- *Ah*, sir," Brady looked beyond the housekeeper and saw his superior descending the stairs, "you need to come quickly, sir. Something terrible's happened."

"I'm sorry about this, Mrs. Wheeler," said Armstrong walking across the hallway, "I'll sort this out. Please go back to bed."

"My giddy aunt!" she mumbled to herself, as she tightened her shawl around her shoulders, "it's a poor do when good honest folk can't get a decent night's sleep." With that she disappeared down the stairs into the basement, from whence she came.

"What is it, Brady?" asked Armstrong.

"There's been a murder, sir, just round on West Walls. You'd better come quick.

Armstrong bolted back up the stairs to his rooms, threw some clothes over his night shirt and hopped into some boots as he made his way toward the stairs once more.

Following the police constable at a half-run, the Inspector reached his subordinate in front of the Abbey Gate, at the north end of the Cathedral. PC Brady pointed along Dean Tait's Lane, and the thirty or so short yards to its junction with West Walls. Armstrong followed the indication. He saw the unmistakable silhouette of another uniformed policemen against the soft light omitted from the gas lamp behind him. But as he approached the scene, Armstrong saw the reason for the commotion: lying in front of the constable was a dark supine figure. Cornelius picked his way carefully on tip-toe over the body, holding on the sides of the lane to steady himself, as he did so. He noticed a middle-aged man sitting on the curb under the street light – he wore the same shocked expression as the two police constables. Turning to look at the body properly for the first time, he saw the reason why.

The victim lay on his back, with his face upturned; his eyes wide open in a mixed expression of horror and, almost, surprise at what had just happened. His dark, handsome, blood-spattered features were gnarled into an incredible facial distortion, while his shoulder-length black hair fanned out from one side of his head. In the darkness, it was difficult to see where the man's hair ended and the trail of dark congealed blood – which ran for over three feet back down the lane – began.

Armstrong stared at the corpse, trying to gather his thoughts. 'When was the body found?' he asked to either of his subordinates.

"About half an hour ago, sir," said Tommy Gibson, who had been guarding the body, while his colleague had gone to wake their superior.

The Inspector instinctively reached for his fob watch before realising that he was virtually half dressed. "It's quarter past twelve, sir," said Gibson. "Mr. Elliot here," he continued, pointing to the man sitting on the curbside "discovered the body when he was on the way home from the pub."

The pubs shut at ten o'clock Armstrong thought but knew it was unimportant. After the fuzziness of the last three hours, he fought to clear his head in order to concentrate on the next few hours: *the Coroner; the Chief Constable; dealing with newspaper men; speaking with the family* – it was going to be a long night. "Do we know who he is?"

"There was a slip in his waistcoat pocket, sir, that made reference to Rucci's Fruit and Vegetable Sales." Gibson handed it over to Armstrong, "I think they have one of the stalls in the market, sir."

Propped up against the wall was a large piece of hardboard about five feet in length by three feet in width, with the top cut diagonally at an angle of about forty-five degrees. "What's that?" asked Armstrong reaching out.

"Careful, sir, it's a bit of a mess."

The Inspector eased it off the wall and looked at the facing side; it was covered in streaks of blood. "Where was this?" he asked.

"Pretty much where it stands, sir. It's almost as though the body's been laying on it. Could it have been used to move the body here from elsewhere?" Armstrong never answered but looked thoughtfully at the sheet of hardboard for a moment.

A handful of people had started to congregate after being drawn by the policeman's whistle that had signalled the emergency.

An upstairs window of the house adjacent to the lane gradually glowed into life, and its luminescent rectangle was soon inhabited by the silhouette of a large man in his nightshirt. It was only at that moment that Armstrong realised that there was the muffled noise of a dog barking. It was now that his foggy state cleared. "We need to get these people away from here and secure the area. Brady, you take Mr. Elliot back to the station; call Sergeant Smith – I know his landlady has a telephone – and get him down here with some more men, and get someone here to take some photographs of the body before it is moved."

"Do you want me to shove a broom up me backside an' all?" Brady mumbled under his breath, thankfully not catching the ear of his superior.

Armstrong then addressed Elliot, "I'm afraid this may take some time, sir. We'll need a statement before you can go."

The passerby shrugged in resignation, "Better off than that poor bugger, I suppose," and followed the uniformed policeman along West Walls towards the station.

"Start moving these people on, Gibson." Armstrong resumed.

"Sir, what about the killer?"

Armstrong turned to look behind him at the steps that led down to the Towndyke Orchard. "I have a feeling he is long gone," he said, almost to himself.

Chapter Three

The Investigation Begins

Having finally got back to his bed around six o'clock, the Inspector was awoken three short hours later, as the Cathedral bells pealed to signify of the imminent morning service. Dragging himself out of bed, Cornelius was back at his desk before the service had finished. He knew that time was precious; it was only hours since the murder but the brutality of the event would mean that news would travel fast around the small city and it would not be long before a quiet Sunday morning would be turned into a frenzied turmoil with newspaper reporters and busybodies sticking their noses into the affair and muddying the waters with their theories and suspicions.

It had been one of his uniformed officers who had retraced the victim's steps that apparently led to his stall at the covered market on Fisher Street. Although most of the stallholders had packed up and left the market for the night, PC Harry Stokes had established from a couple of stragglers that the fruit and veg stall referred to on the card pulled from the young man's pocket was not actually owned by the victim himself, but by his father who lived on Warwick Square with his wife. By the time the same uniformed officer had made it to the Ruccis' home to ask about their son's whereabouts, the grapevine had beaten him to it and the boy's near hysterical parents were hurrying towards the police station in the hope that someone had made a terrible mistake.

They arrived less than ten minutes after the body had been carried the few hundred yards to where it now lay in one of the rooms at the back of the West Walls station. The look of terror and disbelief on the faces of the two immigrants suggested a ghastly inevitability as to what was about to happen. The make-shift cover was drawn back to reveal the blood-caked corpse, with the grievous lesion to its neck. Upon seeing the sunken, pallid face of her son, with his cold, unblinking eyes staring up at her, Signora Rucci let out an ear-piercing scream that was loud and long. Her husband simply collapsed to his knees sobbing uncontrollably into his hands. The boy's mother was inconsolable, *"SALVATORE, SALVATORE MIO FIGLIO BELL,"* she screeched, reaching out as she was helped away, *"IL MIO BAMBINO,"* she cried towards the gathered policemen who looked away in discomfiture.

*****

Several hours later, Inspector Armstrong was now bracing himself to visit the Ruccis to perform one of the hardest jobs faced by any policeman – that of trying to glean information from bereaved and grieving relatives.

When he arrived, he was led into the back kitchen where an eclectic mix of friends and neighbours were trying to comfort the pair. The policeman hovered uncomfortably, shifting the brim of his hat through his fingers. "Excuse me for intruding on your grief," he said, "thank you for agreeing to see me, and let me offer my heartfelt condolences."

Signor Rucci looked at the Inspector blankly, appearing not to hear what was being said, let alone who was saying it. His wife meanwhile didn't acknowledge his presence; she sat clutching her apron, rocking back and forward mumbling in Italian.

"There are some questions I have to ask, sir?" continued Armstrong.

Signor Rucci again showed no comprehension.

Cornelius sat down but decided not to take out his pencil and pad.

"How long have you been in Carlisle, sir?"

Rucci replied in his thick Italian accent, "Only about one year."

"Did you arrive directly from Italy?"

"No, we arrive here from London."

"And how long were you there?"

Rucci seemed to hesitate. "About five years," he said at last.

"May I ask why you came to Carlisle?"

"There are many Italian people coming here, and it is closer to Glasgow where my wife's –" he screwed his face up searching for the word, "- *parents* live."

"How old was your son, Mr. Rucci?"

For the first time, the boy's father met the policeman's gaze, as he used the word 'was'. "Twenty-one," he said with tears in his eyes.

"Have you any idea why someone would want to harm your son?"

At this point Rucci broke down completely and dissolved into tears shaking his head. This only succeeded in exacerbating his wife's condition. The two held each other – inconsolable.

"Mrs. Rucci doesn't speak any English, Inspector," said one of the people present.

"Excuse me," said Armstrong, taking the hint, "I'll see myself out."

His men meanwhile were either carrying out a search of the murder-sight, including scouring the Towndyke Orchard at the base of the steps leading up to West Walls; or were performing the door to door questioning that invariably followed such a serious, if thankfully unusual, crime.

PC Brady started at the top of Abbey Street. Number 2:

"Morning, sir, I'm sorry to trouble you but there was a serious crime committed last night–"

"Aye, one-u-them daft *I*-talians wasn't it?" interrupted the man before the policeman could elaborate. After trying and failing to get a word in edgeways for several minutes of listening to "I know what I would do wid 'em' and 'there only here for our jobs anyway," Brady gave it up as a bad job and moved to the next house.

"Morning luv, sorry to trouble you –"

"Whadthecawme? It's about them daft *I*-talians isn't it?"

Brady rolled his eyes – this was going to be a long and painful morning. And so it went on:

Mr. Hunter at 14 Finkle Street didn't see anything but whilst he had Brady's attention, decided to complain about the ruffians that rolled out of the pubs late at night. Mrs. Nash on the opposite side of Finkle Street, on the other hand, wanted to complain about Mr. Hunter who was always "...peering out of his window in a funny way." Brady decided not to ask Mrs. Nash what she was doing peering out of her window at him; instead he carried on making meaningless notes about seemingly unconnected events.

His colleagues were faring little better: the best Tommy Gibson could do was to establish that the vicar of St Cuthbert's "...unsightly boil was clearing up nicely," while the highlight for Bobby Green was to get an earful from Mrs. Wilkinson of Castle Street who complained about the state of the streets, especially after she had swept up in front of her house.

All the uniformed officers trooped back to the station with the same weary expression. As they entered, one by one, Inspector Armstrong looked for some cause for optimism – he didn't find any. The only straws to cling on to were the four addresses where the policemen received no replies – two on Annettwell Street and one each on Blackfriars Street and Atkinson's Court.

That night Cornelius met his cousin and best friend George Armstrong for their usual Sunday night drink in *The Board Inn* on the corner of Paternoster Row and Castle Street. George was a Sergeant in the Border Regiment and – as the regiment was stationed at the castle since their return from the war in South Africa – billeted in the barracks on Annettwell Street.

"I'm struggling, George," said the policeman as the two Armstrongs sat in a booth in the busy pub, over a pint of beer and a whiskey chaser.

"You've got to trust yourself, Corny," reassured his cousin. "You're a damn good copper; the best old Baker's got – and he knows it. He wouldn't have put you on the case to start with if he didn't think you were up to it."

"He doesn't have a lot of choice: there's old Parker, who's been winding down to retirement for the past thirty years; and then there's that waste-of-space Robinson – he couldn't catch a cold if he was sitting in a draft, let alone catch a brutal killer threatening to terrorise the city. Besides it only happened last night and it was almost on my doorstep. I've no motive, no weapon and no killer. If things don't come together soon, I'll be given the old heave-ho and the Scotland Yarders will be in before you know it."

"It's so unusual for Carlisle," said George, thinking aloud. "Does that rogue from Caldewgate, not know anything?"

"Hanks? I haven't spoken to him yet. But you're right; it just doesn't seem like Carlisle. There was no sign of any disturbance – the body just lay there on its own. No one saw anything, no one heard anything. And the fact that the boy was Italian suggests there's something more to this than meets the eye."

"How long has he been in Carlisle?"

"A year," answered Cornelius.

"From what you tell me it seems as though the boy was being chased towards the police station."

"It seems that way but he has been attacked from the front."

"There may have been two of them," speculated George.

"Umm," nodded his cousin, "that would make sense. One would chase the lad knowing he would head for the station on West Walls, while the other hid in the shadows at the end of the lane waiting for him."

"What time do you think it happened?" asked the soldier.

Cornelius sat back in his seat, tilted his head back and exhaled in resignation. The picture hanging above the booth at which they were sitting caught his eye. This, coupled with his cousin's most recent question seemed to spark a realisation in the Police Inspector. "Of course," he said, still looking at the picture. George looked up and saw the image of a steam locomotive at Carlisle Station. "The time and the location could be significant," continued Cornelius, "not because it was quiet, but – assuming for a moment the killers weren't from Carlisle – they could catch the sleeper south within a few minutes of murdering the boy. We reckon he was killed about quarter to midnight – I'm sure the sleeper leaves about five-to. If this is right, it would give them just enough time to make their way along Damside and on to the train. Thanks George," said a perked up policeman, patting his cousin on the shoulder, "you've been a great help."

Chapter Four

A Sinister Arrival

"**W**HAT?"

"HAVE YOU SEEN ..." Armstrong paused as the noise from stream engine abated, "Have you seen any unusual activity or any unusual characters around the station during the last few days?"

Harold Irving, Platform Supervisor for many a long year, looked at the Inspector quizzically. "How do you mean?"

The cavernous interior of Citadel Station glowed in the morning sunshine like an enormous blacksmith's forge. The intense noise from engines, whistles and clattering rails made Inspector Armstrong's job even harder than it already was.

"I mean ... " as he was about to elaborate, a signalman blasted on his whistle and a goods train heaved its way from the platform where Armstrong was trying to interview the railway man ... "I MEAN CAN YOU REMEMBER ANY PARTICULAR DIST ... disturbances that seemed out of the ordinary. Were there any ... WERE THERE ANY ..." This was ridiculous. When there was a suitable moment Armstrong asked if there was somewhere they could go that afforded a little less chance of being disturbed. Irving gestured to the signalman further down the platform that he was taking the policeman up a flight of stairs into what turned out to be a bothy where the staff seemed to retire for a break.

"Can I get you a cuppa?" asked Irving politely.

"No thank you," replied Armstrong, keen to advance his investigation. "You probably know about the murder on Saturday night?"

"Oh-aye, nasty business. Never trust them daft *I*-talians, me."

"What could be significant is the time of the killing – just before midnight. Could I ask what time the sleeper leaves Carlisle?"

"Four minutes to midnight," replied Irving.

"Four minutes to," repeated Cornelius to himself, "is that also on a Saturday?"

"Every night."

"Do you know if it left on time Saturday gone?" asked the policeman.

The railway man looked a little piqued by a question which suggested that late trains were a regular occurrence. He disappeared into an adjacent office and returned within a few minutes. "Bang on time, as usual," he took great delight in announcing.

"Is there any way of checking the passengers who got on the train?"

"The only way is to check the ticket book and see if anyone booked a berth."

Irving obligingly disappeared again. "The only people booked on the sleeper were a Mr. & Mrs. James Wainwright – according to one-eyed Jimmy," he added, gesticulating over his shoulder towards the office from whence he came, "they were a couple of newly-weds travelling down to Brighton for their honeymoon. Honestly, I don't know how he finds all this out but it'll be right if old 'one-eye' says so. God help us all if the bugger had two."

"But that's just from Carlisle?" asked Armstrong, trying to pull the conversation back to the matter at hand.

"That's right. If someone bought a return from elsewhere there would be no way of knowing."

"Where does the sleeper stop?"

"Just here and Preston before London."

"What about Friday or Saturday, Harold? Did you see anything or anyone unusual in or around the station? Strangers perhaps?" No sooner had Armstrong asked the question when he recognised how ridiculous it must have sounded.

"This is a railway station Inspector," said the Platform Supervisor, "I see strangers every day coming off the trains." He thought awhile. "The only thing I can offer is that there was something on Friday afternoon on Platform 4 with the quarter-to-twelve train from Glasgow. A couple of young blokes had had too much to drink by the time the train reached Carlisle and the guard called me on to the train to escort them off and into the custody of your railway colleagues. By the time we got them off the train they were getting a bit boisterous."

Armstrong knew there was little value in delving further into this incident as it seemed highly unlikely that it could be connected to his investigation. He thanked Mr. Irving and told him that if there was anything he – or his disabled, yet well-informed colleague – could remember he should contact him immediately. With that, he left the station a little crestfallen but not unsurprised by the fruitlessness of his visit.

What Armstrong had remained unaware of – as had Harold Irving for that matter – was that as the Platform Supervisor was attending to the two ruffians on Platform 4 that Friday afternoon, unknown to him, a tall dark figure stepped down from the Glasgow-*bound* train on Platform 1 at the other side of the station. Crossing the bridge towards the exit he stopped a porter making the opposite journey towards the northbound platform. "Could you tell me where I can get some digs?" he asked.

"There's a hotel just outside the station, sir," replied the porter.

"No, somewhere quieter," he said, scanning his surroundings, almost ignoring the young man who was trying to help him.

The porter thought for a few seconds. "You'll get a room at Joe Fargie's – a lot of the railway lads stay there when they have an overnighter. Just go across the square to the left and follow your nose down English Damside to the orchard; then up the steps on to West Walls and Joe's place is a hundred yards along at Atkinson's Court. You'll be alright there." The stranger barely acknowledged the lad as he walked off. "You're welcome," said the youngster, understandably chagrined.

As he descended the steps heading for the exit, he saw a station official struggling to contain two men whose raised voices were causing quite a scene. Ignoring the fracas, he followed the porter's directions, walking across Court Square and down the sweeping English Damside that was a natural canyon with its high station walls on one side and the dour, imposing gaol on the other. After a few hundred yards he came to Towndyke Orchard and looked across to his right to see an eight-foot wide walkway at the base of the wall; further along the walkway was a stone stairway to West Walls – a lane that took its self explanatory name from the western perimeter of the city. He stopped and looked across at the steps; and then over his shoulder at his trodden path. He smiled crookedly to himself; "Just about perfect," he mumbled.

Joseph Ferguson – or Old Joe Fargie as everyone knew him – was a retired railway worker himself. Widowed twice, he now lived on his own with his little dog within sight and sound of the rattle and clatter of the trains that accelerated away from, and decelerated into his old place of work. The noise somehow gave him some comfort. He earned a few bob by renting out the one spare room he had in his tenement on Atkinson's Court.

It was about three o'clock when the old man was having his usual doss in the chair, with his black pug sleeping in its basket beside him, when there was a loud rap on the door. Shaking himself awake, he had just about levered himself out of his chair when the knock was repeated – longer and louder.

"A'right, a'right, I'm coming," Joe shouted before dissolving into a coughing fit.

Finally making it to the door, he beheld a tall man with a large carpet bag and a face that was partially obscured by his cap that was pulled down. "You have a room?" he asked without pleasantries.

"Aye, three-n-six a night," said Joe turning to show his new lodger to his billet. The two walked in file up two flights of the dusty staircase towards the single door on the top landing; half way up the second flight, the landlord's breathing started to fail him, causing him to lean against the wall. "If I'd known you were coming," he wheezed, "I'd have left the key under the mat and set off yesterday to meet you here!" Joe laughed a smoker's throaty laugh – looking out of the corner of his eye however he saw no flicker of amusement on the face of his guest.

Joe made it up the final few steps and opened the door: it was dark and basic. Again, the expression on the stranger's face didn't change but his host sensed his lack of enthusiasm.

"Not what you're used to?" enquired the old man still catching his breath after the long haul up the stairs. His guest didn't answer. "Come far?" he persisted.

"Three-n-six," replied the stranger pushing the appropriate coins into the old man's hand, while using his large frame to usher his host towards the door.

It slammed shut, leaving Joe on the landing alone. "Bloody Southerners," he cackled to himself as he prepared his treacherous descent.

Chapter Five

Searching For Witnesses

Cornelius sat back in his chair, absentmindedly rubbing the bristles on the top of his closely cropped head with the palm of his hand; he was becoming increasingly convinced that Rucci's killer was not from the city. But what did he have to go on? Just his intuition, that's what – and that would hardly placate the press, public or his boss.

He arranged to wire his colleague Inspector Daniel Standish in Preston, to ask for assistance with his theory: had anything happened in or around the station on Friday or especially during the early hours of Sunday morning, regarding the Glasgow to London sleeper?

The previous month, Armstrong had also exchanged some telephone calls with Inspector Tobias Gregson of Scotland Yard, concerning a gang of London villains, one of whom was locked up in Carlisle Gaol. Armstrong decided to drop the obliging Gregson a line also, explaining his predicament and theory.

He then, levered himself into his overcoat once more and grabbed his bowler, informing the Duty Sergeant, Bill Townsend, that he was going to the Market to see if any of Rucci's fellow stall holders could shed any light on the events.

It had seemed a mild, pleasant morning when he walked the short distance to work earlier, but now the day had deteriorated rapidly; heavy clouds scurried across the sky and a fierce blustery wind whistled down West Walls. Armstrong

29

reversed what he believed to be Salvatore Rucci's final steps three days earlier: *back down Dean Tait's Lane; then where? Along Paternoster Row and down Long Lane on to Fisher Street? Or through the Cathedral grounds and down St Mary's Gate? Had to be the Cathedral – it's quicker.*

At the entrance to the Market on Fisher Street was an open brazier around which a woman, a young girl – apparently her daughter – and two men were huddled. The adults instantly recognised the approaching policeman and almost involuntarily stood up straight. "Morning sir," said one of the men.

"How are you all doing?" said Cornelius as he stopped to benefit from the fire.

"Very well, sir, very well. You'll be here lookin' at this I-talian business nay doubt?"

"That's right," said the Inspector rubbing his hands together and holding them to the fire. "Were any of you here on Saturday night?"

"Our Maggie was," said the other man indicating to the woman.

"And did you see anything, Maggie," asked Armstrong.

"I was standing here with Lizzie Thomson sir, and all of a sudden, there was a right carry-on. The doors bust open and the young boy cem running out; he nearly had the fire over. I remember saying to Lizzie 'he'll catch his death-o-cold that boy,' he only had his shirt on, no coat – in this weather!"

"Do you know what time this was?"

"It must have been late on, sir coz everyone was just about packed up and away."

"What were you and Lizzie doing here so late?"

"We can always get hold of a cheap bit a meat and maybe a few veg at that time-a-night. These bairns won't feed the'sels y'know," she added indignantly, pointing to the child, whose sunken cheeks confirmed that malnutrition was a constant threat to the lives of her class.

"I know," acknowledged Cornelius with a smile, remembering his own upbringing. "Tell me, did you see anyone chasing the lad, or anyone else knocking about who you didn't like the look of?"

"No, sir, we hadn't been here very long but there was nobody after 'im."

"Thanks, Maggie," said the policeman, "that's really helpful." He nodded to her to companions and slipped a sixpence into the palm of the child with a wink. "You look after yourselves now," he said as he pulled open one of the giant doors of the covered market.

Once inside, the aromas of fresh food and the noise of dozens of people buying, selling and haggling turned the otherwise cold hollow building into a hustling and bustling hive of activity.

It wasn't long before Inspector Armstrong discovered the Rucci's fruit and vegetable stall – it was conspicuous by the green tarpaulin sheets that covered it; it stood idle in complete incongruity with the goings-on around it.

Samuel Kelly was a butcher who had the stall directly opposite. Armstrong waited politely while he served a customer. "I wonder if you could tell me anything about Mr. Rucci?" he asked finally.

Kelly, a barrel-chested middle aged man, wore an expression that was as tired as the apron he wore under his jacket. "Not much really. He hasn't been here that long, 'bout twelve months I think. Doesn't know much about fruit-n-veg if y'ask me. I know good Carlisle lads who would run that stall but it ends up with one o' them *I*-talians. That boy of his wasn't' much better when he arrived – wouldn't have him sweepin' the floor, me," he said twisting his mouth to one side in a sarcastic grin. When the Inspector did not smile back, he added with indifference, "still, probably didn't deserve what he got."

Armstrong's piercing blue eyes stared hard at the butcher, "Probably not, Mr. *Kelly*," he repeated nonplussed. "With a name like Kelly I would've thought you would be a bit more tolerant of incomers."

Armstrong's maternal grandparents had immigrated to the city from Ireland like thousands of others in the previous century; he assumed that the butcher's heritage was the same. Kelly seemed to get the message and suddenly saw something of interest on his shoes.

"Did you see any strangers talking to Rucci on Saturday?" resumed the policeman. At this point, a young girl appeared at the edge of a canvass screen to the rear of Kelly's stall. Armstrong instinctively looked across and Kelly turned to see what had attracted his attention. The girl looked from the policeman to her employer and quickly disappeared behind the screen. Cornelius looked back at the butcher who refused to meet his gaze.

"No," said Kelly.

"What did you mean when you said 'when *he* arrived'?"

"Well he's only shown his face in the last few weeks."

"Since his arrival, are both Mr. Rucci and his son here all the time?"

"Usually, but I've noticed the boy's been shutting up himself the last two or three Friday and Saturday nights. I think he was on his own last Saturday."

"Thank you for your time," concluded the Inspector, who was now keen to resume his interview with the victim's parents.

Once at the Warwick Square home of the bereaved parents, Armstrong observed that Mrs. Rucci's mourning went further than the clothes she wore. Hers was the countenance one would expect to see in such dire circumstances: ashen and bewildered by grief. Her husband wore the same blank expression Armstrong had noted two days earlier.

"I'm sorry to intrude again," said the Inspector, "but there are some more questions I would like to ask."

"Can't you just leave us alone, Inspector?" said Rucci

"Sir, we need to find who did this to your son, and the best chance we have is if we move quickly." The Italian didn't respond, but merely offered his guest a chair.

"Can I just ask again how long have you been in Carlisle?"

"I told you the other day, about one year," Rucci was struggling to hide his frustration.

"And when you came," continued Armstrong, "did Salvatore come with you?" Although she spoke no English, the mention of her son's name visibly affected Mrs. Rucci.

"My son has not long arrived in Carlisle,"' said her husband.

"May I ask why he didn't come with you originally?"

"He preferred to stay in London with family."

"So why did he join you eventually?"

"He was missing his mother," said Rucci.

Armstrong looked from one to the other, uncomfortable with his line of questioning and even more uncomfortable with the less than helpful answers. "Do you mind if I look at his room," he asked, hoping to find inspiration elsewhere. The boy's father shrugged and led the policeman upstairs.

The room was non-descript, there was virtually nothing to personalise it. Armstrong silently sought permission to explore the bedside cabinet; Rucci acquiesced with a nod. The policeman opened the predictably untidy draw: a newspaper, a small amount of money, a few scraps of paper with scribbles on them, and an envelope containing a letter written in Italian. He looked at the back of the envelope. "Fabio Palletti, 103 Abbeyfield Road, Rotherhithe," he read, "Do you know this man, Mr. Rucci?"

Rucci hesitated, "Yes, I think Salvatore has mentioned him before. I think they are friends."

Armstrong flipped the envelope back over and noted the postmark that was dated 20th October. "Do you mind if I take these items away, sir? They may be of little use but I would like to look at them further if I may."

Again, Rucci gave a resigned shrug, apparently relieved that agreeing to the policeman's request would once more give him and his wife some peace and quiet. Armstrong took a brown envelope from his inside pocket and placed the letter and the scraps of paper inside. "My apologies once more, Mr. Rucci," he said at the bottom of the stairs, "I will keep you informed of our investigation." He looked through at Mrs. Rucci who was still sitting in the kitchen, but with a glance from her husband, Armstrong decided not to prolong his visit unnecessarily.

Chapter Six

The Italian Connection

"I need some answers, Cornelius." Chief Constable Henry Baker sat in his chair with the air of a troubled man.

"I feel we're making progress, Henry, but it is complicated and slow going." No sooner had Inspector Armstrong arrived back at the station, when he had been summoned to his superior's office.

The Chief Constable took out his pocket watch – it was just after four o'clock. "Jack Dixon from the *Journal* has asked to see me at half past for an update. The damn newspapers are already enjoying this out-of-the-ordinary affair. I don't want them filling up their columns with fanciful speculation. That other obnoxious character from the *Patriot* even had the temerity to ask yesterday if the job was too big for us – would we be 'bringing the Scotland Yarders in?' What *can* I tell them?"

The two had spent almost twenty years together on the local force and had a close relationship but Armstrong sensed the strain was beginning to tell on his boss and decided to cease with his informal approach. "It's just too complex at the moment, sir. You could hold them off by informing them that the postmortem will be carried out this afternoon – we will perhaps know more then." Baker looked at Armstrong sceptically, prompting the latter to continue. "The lad appears to have been frightened by something or someone – enough to send him scurrying here, but of course, he never made it. I'm beginning to think that the killer or killers weren't local and there's some connection from elsewhere."

"*Killers*?" repeated Baker emphasising the plural.

"Well it's just one theory, sir. The boy seems to have been attacked from the front, which suggests that someone was waiting for him at that point. Why would they chase him down the narrow lane, then overtake him, and then kill him?"

"He could've have been killed elsewhere," suggested the senior policeman.

"I don't think so sir. His injuries created so much blood there would surely've been a trail. There wasn't a spot of blood anywhere outside a four foot radius of the body. I just think there's more to this than meets the eye."

"What makes you think that?"

"Well, the family haven't been in Carlisle very long and the boy's been here even less. I'm just wondering if he's been running away from something." After allowing this to sink in with his boss, the detective added, "I also think the timing and the location is important. The killing seems to have taken place between half past eleven and a quarter to twelve. The south-bound sleeper left Carlisle at four minutes to midnight; I think it's possible that they could have killed the lad and dashed down the steps, through the orchard and onto the train. I've contacted Inspectors at Preston and London to see if they can help with this theory."

Baker shifted uncomfortably in his chair. "Theories are all well and good, Cornelius, but we need some hard facts. I can hold the papers at bay for another few days but if we don't see some results soon, there'll be questions asked of us. I don't want to come across as a bunch of small-town bumpkins who don't know what they're doing. We could end up a laughing stock if we're not careful."

Armstrong left the Chief Constable to handle the newspaper man and decided there was little more he could do here; he collected what evidence he had – the letter and the papers – and opted to pour over them at home. Standing at the murder site again, the policeman tried to envisage the killing once more. *Who was he running from?* And then out loud to himself, "What had this boy been up to?"

"What's that sir?" said a voice nearby.

Armstrong looked up to see the lamplighter at work along West Walls. "Hello, Bobby. Nothing, I'm just driving myself barmy that's all."

Bobby Lloyd was a well-known, jovial character who had arrived in Carlisle from Liverpool some years earlier with the coming of the railways. He had since established a comfortable job for himself as a lamplighter in and around the city centre. His thick Liverpool accent, quick-fire humour and propensity to laugh at his own jokes made him both an amusing and popular figure. "If only I could shed some light on the situation, for you," he said followed by his staccato laugh.

"I wish it were that simple, Bobby, lad," said the policemen, getting the joke and appreciating some light relief, "but I just don't understand it," he added half to himself.

"You know what I don't understand?" before Cornelius could respond, Bobby delivered the punch-line *"Chinese writing!"* More laughter.

"You should be in the circus, Bobby, lad."

"Did you hear about the fire in the circus? *It was intense!"*

Shaking his head, the Inspector conceded defeat and turned to walk along the lane, "Mind how you go, Bobby," he said with a smile.

With the key in the door to 22A Abbey Street, Cornelius suddenly had a thought to visit the Tullie House Library opposite Although he himself had an extensive collection of books, he didn't know very much about Italian culture; he knew he was potentially clutching at another straw but maybe there was something on the library shelves that could give him a glimmer of hope. As luck would have it, the Librarian Sydney Irvine provided four volumes that detailed, "...the history, traditions and culture of Italy. We ordered them especially from the British Library Mr. Armstrong. As more and more Italians seem to be coming to Carlisle, we hope that they will start using Tullie House." Cornelius thought of Mrs. Rucci who didn't speak a word of English, and then about Italians in general who presumably knew about their history, traditions and culture; he decided not to dampen the Librarian's enthusiasm however, and simply thanked him for his help.

After young Emma Wheeler had cleared away the dishes from his evening meal, Cornelius lit a paraffin lamp and settled down at his desk to pore over the information that would hopefully unlock the mystery. The letter from Salvatore's friend – obviously written in Italian – was brief: it scarcely covered one side of notepaper. That notwithstanding, the only things the detective could decipher were the date – 20th Ottobre 1903 – two weeks before the murder, and three asterisks that punctuated the text at various points.

Sitting back in his chair Armstrong lit his long stemmed cherry-wood pipe and stared blankly at the letter: *was there any significance in the date and its close proximity to Rucci's murder? And what words were those asterisks replacing?* "Again Corny lad," he said himself, "too many questions, not enough answers."

Instead of dwelling on the note, he turned his attention to the library books hoping they might provide some inspiration. Skimming through them, Armstrong noted information about ancient Rome, opera and the favourite food of the country: pasta, dry or fresh dough that is usually served with sauce or seasonings. Much as he loved history, music and food, this was getting him nowhere. The only thing Cornelius found moderately interesting was a piece about social change in the century just past and how the increased north-south divide had led to a growth in organised gangs in the south of the country. He read with interest that:

> ... in the latter half of the century organised gangs sprung throughout the Campania region of southern Italy and on the island of Sicily. Each group, known as a clan or 'cosca' claims sovereignty over a territory in which it carries out smuggling, blackmailing and the demanding of

money from businesses in exchange for the service of 'protection' against crimes that the gangs themselves instigate if unpaid.

The Sicilian criminal societies have become known as Mafia and include the now infamous coscas of Villalba, Mussomeli and Corleonesi, who take their names from their founder members; all Mafia coscas have developed a hierarchical pyramid structure.

Centered around the city of Naples on the mainland however, exists the equally violent and frightening Camorra. Their coscas have less structure, which results in many clans acting independently of each other and inevitably feuding amongst themselves. Prominent among the Camorra are the more glamorously named Il Rosso circolo (The Red Circle), Il Cinque Punti (The Five Points) and Apprendisti di Napoli (The Apprentices of Naples)

In reading about the gang violence, Cornelius afforded himself a smile at the similarities between the nineteenth century Italian version and that of their seventeenth century Borders' counterparts, from whom he himself was descended on his father's side. For the Mafia's Villalba, Mussomeli and Corleonesi, he thought, you could easily substitute the Reivers' Armstrongs, Elliots and Grahams.

Straining his tired eyes, it was proving a long night for the Inspector who, all the while, couldn't help wondering how the postmortem had gone that afternoon. Finally, after over three hours of tying himself in Italian knots, he moved to his chair by the fire and opted instead for some of Charles Dickens's work, which, he hoped, would provide some much needed entertainment and distraction. But after only a few pages he realised he was taking nothing in; the elaborate case of Jarndyce and Jarndyce couldn't distract the policeman from the complexity of his own inquiries. After putting off the inevitable, he chose to turn in around midnight, knowing full well he had a restive night ahead of him.

Chapter Seven

The Informant

Grateful to be out of the icy room of death and back into the fresh air, and armed with Dr. Bell's large brown envelope, with his findings from the postmortem, Inspector Armstrong decided to walk from the hospital to the station through Caldewgate, the Irish Quarter of Carlisle. It was an area he knew well having been brought up there and he knew he could run an errand along the way. Wednesday morning was Market Day throughout the city and the unimaginatively named 'Paddy's Market' was in full swing on Bridge Street as Armstrong walked down the hill passed Trinity Church.

By eleven o'clock the pavements were crowded with shoppers, bustling around the stalls and jostling under awnings, looking for affordable produce.

As the policeman walked deeper into the market, the air became filled with the babble of the noisy crowd. He felt rather conspicuous as he picked his way between women in shawls haggling with the stall holders over poultry, eggs and pork.

He couldn't find the man he was looking for and didn't want to unnecessarily prolong his search. He turned to cut through an alleyway of canopied stalls; as he did so, he heard the unmistakably gruff voice, he had been hoping for: '...and before I knew it, the bugger 'ad med off wid me bloody dog!' Armstrong smiled to himself. At the next junction of stalls, he saw a stoutly built man who wore an old brown frock-coat that had long seen better days. Scuffed boots at one end and a frayed seaman's cap at the other gave him all the appearance of one of life's hard knocks. He was reciting his tale of woe to an elderly women with a wicker basket full of produce; she seemed happy to prolong the conversation by interspersing the odd 'well I never,' and 'I don't know what the world's coming to.'

"Hello, Reuben," interrupted the Inspector, as the man came into view.

"Mr. Armstrong, sir!" A look of incredulity covered the man's face, before the sudden realisation of being seen speaking to a policeman dawned. He looked furtively from side to side and almost involuntarily dipped his head into his shoulders. "You shouldn't come here, sir."

"I need your help, Reuben."

"Just not here, sir." I'll be in the 'Blazing Barrel' tonight at seven o'clock. With a nod of assent from the policeman, the ruffian scuttled away into the crowd, leaving his companion in a state of bewilderment. Cornelius meanwhile marched off in the opposite direction towards the police station on the other side of the city walls.

"Any chance of a cup of tea?" he shouted through to PC Brady as he removed his hat and coat.

"Right away, sir," came the muffled response from the mess room at the bottom of the corridor.

While Brady searched among the enamel mugs on the drainer for one least likely to poison his superior, Armstrong settled down at his desk and opened the thick brown envelope. The Inspector skimmed through the contents: a hand-written report on the findings of the autopsy, details of its sequence, and a series of photographs of the cadaver taken during the procedure.

Armstrong twisted the horns of his moustache and stared at the photographs. An incision had been made from the victim's larynx to his abdomen and the skin and superficial layers of tissue had been peeled back. The pictures were not particularly clear, most were dark and grainy; despite this, the man's glistening organs could be seen as the pathologist shone a light into the raw, empty cavity of Rucci's torso.

Brady disturbed the Inspector's concentration by knocking and entering with his drink. "Is this tea?" asked Armstrong suspiciously, peering into the black liquid – he gurned after the first mouthful.

"If you say so, sir," replied Brady on his way out.

"No wonder folk get badly round here," grumbled Armstrong to himself. The pathologist's appalling handwriting made his report a difficult one to read: '*A cut was made above the larynx, detaching the larynx and* – the something or other – *from the* – I can't make that out either.' He persevered as best he could: '*The larynx and ... are then pulled downward, and the scalpel is used to free up the remainder of the chest organs from their attachment at the spine...examined the interior...thyroid gland is dissected...weighed, and examined in thin slices.*' The only other thing Armstrong could make out was a reference to '*...an unconnected raw wound just above the boy's left shoulder blade.*' He took another sip of tea and squirmed at its bitterness.

Just then, Chief Constable Baker came in – a clear sign that he wanted to be kept updated at every stage, "Have you been to the hospital?" he asked.

"I have, sir, I'm just going through the postmortem findings now."

Baker picked up the photographs on Armstrong's desk. "What did Bell say?"

"He said that the boy had been 'executed' by someone who knew exactly what he was doing?"

The Chief Constable looked from the photographs to Armstrong without moving; the two exchanged a tacit recognition that they were in danger of losing control of the case. "What's our next move?" asked Baker.

"I'm still waiting on any reply from Standish or Gregson about my train theory. As far as local involvement is concerned, I'm meeting someone tonight – if anyone will know, he will."

The senior policeman tossed the photographs back on the desk and turned to leave, "We need something firm by tomorrow, Cornelius. Otherwise, I'll be contacting Scotland Yard."

"Understood, sir."

The Old Black Bull Inn on Annettwell Street had a large barrel above the door, which was in fact a big illuminated gas light. It therefore had the nickname, 'The Blazing Barrel'. At the appointed hour Inspector Armstrong met the man he had sought out earlier that day.

Like Cornelius Armstrong, Reuben Hanks had been born and raised in Caldewgate. Unlike Armstrong, Hanks had not set out to educate and better himself by reading, writing and establishing a reputable career that demanded respect and admiration. Instead, Reuben had explored life on the other side of the tracks, which, in turn, had previously led to activity on the other side of the law. Ironic then that the two would follow completely different paths but invariably end up at the same point, with the policeman – then a uniformed constable or sergeant – arresting the scallywag Hanks for his various misdemeanors. Now, after more than ten years – and with Cornelius advancing his career to Detective Inspector – the two had developed a more amicable arrangement that saw the labourer help out the policeman from time to time in return for Armstrong giving him a little less attention when it came to some of his own questionable activities.

Armstrong had already bought the ale and was sitting in a booth when Reuben entered; Hanks sat down, drew a sleeve across his nose, pulled the cap from his head and ran his bunchy fingers through his greasy, tousled hair. "You're a gent Mr. Armstrong, sir," he said tipping his tankard back until rivulets of liquid runnelled down his unshaven chin. He replaced the tankard carelessly, slopping some of the contents onto the table. Leaning forward, into the light, his features could now be seen clearly: he had a tough face with a beard of several days' growth that partially masked a scar that ran diagonally under his nose and across his lips. He looked at the policeman with his scowling eyes. "Is it about this *I*-talian bloke, sir?" he asked, taking a dirty paisley handkerchief from around his neck and wiping beer from his face.

Armstrong took a gulp of his own tankard and swiftly removed any excess liquid from both sides of his mustache with a continuous swirling motion of the back of his index finger, "Yes, I don't mind telling you I'm pretty desperate – I don't suppose you've heard anything?"

"Well, it's the talk of the place as ye might imagine but that's not to say anybody knows owt about it."

"Do you know anything about this bloke Elliot who discovered the body?"

"Oh, I wouldn't concern yoursel' with him, sir, he's a right heed-the-ba' – couldn't find his own arse with both hands. Mind you, he has a house full of bairns down Wapping so he must be good at summut."

"What about Kelly the butcher in the market? He seems a strange fella."

"Yeah – *bloody* strange. I've had a few run-ins wid him when he comes down to Paddy's Market. He doesn't think twice about flogging slink or auld meat that's riddled wid broxy."

"Do you think he's capable of being involved in something like this? It's clear he doesn't like the Italians or the Ruccis in particular – he didn't seem very keen on helping when I spoke to him."

"I don't think so, Mr. Armstrong. He might be a miserable bugger but I don't think he's capable of doing summut like this – and another thing, he's too tight-fisted to pay for somebody else to do it an' all," added Hanks with a smile.

"Did I see a young lass working for him?" asked Cornelius.

"Yeah, it's young Rose Green; she's a smart la'al lass. Lives with her father down in Poet's Corner. I wouldn't be surprised if the young swarthy *I*-talian didn't make friends wid her – it might be worth having a chat."

"That's a good idea, Reuben," said Armstrong, writing down the girl's address, "I think I'll do that."

He thanked his contact for his help and walked towards the door; as he did so he heard an acquaintance of Hanks shout over to him, "Oi, Reuben, are you sorting out that sweep you were on about yesterday?" Hanks quickly looked over to the departing policeman, hoping that he hadn't heard; Armstrong momentarily stopped but decided to simply return a glance that was half-amusement, half- disapproval at hearing of the illegal, if common act in most public houses. Reuben looked suitably guilty, but shrugged philosophically at Cornelius, who left him to it.

Chapter Eight

The Breakthrough

Cornelius Armstrong knew Caldewgate, and particularly Poet's Corner well. Byron, Shakespeare and Milton all had streets named after them which inevitably led to the colloquial nickname given to the pocket of streets behind *The Joiners' Arms*, or 'Blue Lugs' as it was known because of the blue veins that were visible in the oversized ears of the unfortunate landlord.

The Inspector picked his way through the labyrinthine alleyways, with their seemingly endless squalid dwellings, until he came to a narrow gap between two terraced houses on Milton Street; through it he went, and found himself in a long dark, dank lane. Drooped across the lane were two washing lines from which – despite the early hour – a few damp shirts and underclothes hung sadly.

All was silent at this early hour, except for the flurry of an occasional rat, as it scurried back and forth from one side of the lane to the other. Cornelius picked his way along the lane and up an open stone stair to a first floor tenement where the odorous, unmistakable smells of damp washing and boiled cabbage instantly triggered childhood memories of his own upbringing on Henderson Square, just off Byron Street. He took out the piece of paper and checked the address he had written down the night before in the Blazing Barrel and knocked.

Rose Green was eighteen, red-headed and pretty; she lived

with her widowed father. She had obtained a position as Assistant Butcher to Samuel Kelly at the Whitsun hirings in May; initially for six months but her hard work and dedication had led to an extension, and saved her employer the trouble of recruiting again at the Martinmas hirings only two weeks earlier.

When there was a knock at the door, she was standing at the sink washing some pots before going to work. She opened the door and was visibly shocked to see a smartly dressed, groomed man standing on her step.

"Rose? My name is Cornelius Armstrong, I'm a policeman."

Recognition registered with the young girl who had seen the Inspector interviewing her employer earlier that week. The recognition however, did not assuage feelings of surprise and possibly even guilt at the Police Inspector visiting her home. "I don't understand, sir," she stammered.

"It's alright, Rose, you're not in any trouble. I was just hoping you could help me with some questions about the young Italian lad, that's all."

"You best come in then, sir," said Rose with some relief, "although we'll need to keep our voices down because me Dad was in late last night and is still in bed," she gestured towards the other room.

Cornelius removed his hat and Rose indicated a chair in the austere room that afforded virtually no natural light. Speaking in a hushed tone he asked, "How long have you worked for Mr. Kelly?"

"Since the hirings in May," replied the young girl.

"Do you like the job?"

Rose smiled awkwardly; Cornelius guessed that hers wasn't the nicest employer one could encounter. "It's alright," she said simply.

"Did you know Salvatore Rucci, Rose?"

"A little bit, he was nice and polite."

"Could you say how long he has worked on his father's stall?"

Rose thought for a while, "Not long," she said, "only a couple-o-months I would say."

"Did he ever tell you why he came to Carlisle?"

"No, he liked to come over and talk to me when Mr. Kelly wasn't about but when he showed up, he would chase Sal off. He didn't like him, and he didn't like me talkin' to him neither."

"Can you remember anything about Saturday? Did you see anything unusual? Anything out the ordinary?"

Armstrong was surprised by the swiftness of Rose's response, "There was a man who put a piece of paper under some crates by the Rucci's stall."

The Inspector locked onto this information and pressed the young girl trying not to intimidate her in the process. "Had you ever seen the man before? Maybe a regular customer?"

"No."

"What did he look like?"

"He was a big bloke, tall. He was wearing a black coat and hat..." it was the best she could do as she tailed off the description with a shrug.

"Did he speak to Salvatore?"

"No, I was watching him for a bit. He waited till Sal left his stall to help the barrow boy load up and then put something under the crates. It was like he was hiding it 'cause Sal wouldn't have cleared the empties away till later."

"Do you know why Salvatore was on his own on Saturday?"

"For the past two or three weeks, he's run the stall his sel' on a Saturday. He told me that it gives his dad a break, that's all."

"Did you see if Salvatore picked up the paper?"

"No, I left about seven o'clock. I was gonna tell him but Mr. Kelly had 'is beady eyes on me and I didn't get the chance. By the time I left, I'd forgot about it."

"Thank you Rose, you've been extremely helpful."

Armstrong left Rose feeling he had the beginnings of a breakthrough. *Who was this stranger? Why did he visit Rucci without speaking to him? And what did he hide? The boy was murdered the same night - this is surely more than coincidence.*

No sooner had he arrived at his desk than the duty sergeant blundered into his office, "Sir, there is an urgent telephone call from the Inspector at Preston."

Armstrong hurried through to the front office and grabbed the ear-piece that lay on the desk with one hand and picked up the candlestick telephone with the other. "Inspector Standish?.... Yes....Where was it found?.... What was in it?...It has to be, I would like to come down and pick it up this afternoon."

"Sir?" questioned Sergeant Townsend.

"They've found a bag near the railway line outside Preston," said Armstrong without elaborating, "I'm going down there now to pick it up. Where's Sergeant Smith?" without waiting for an answer, he called out down the corridor, before going to retrieve his hat and coat, "*SMITH?*"

The gangly Detective Sergeant lumbered into his superior's office a few seconds later, "Sir?"

"I want you to take a couple of men down to the Market and search Rucci's stall again. You're looking for a piece of discarded paper or an envelope. I'll be back later this afternoon." With that, he was gone, dashing off towards the station. Sergeant Smith stood in the Inspector's office thankful he was in such a hurry – otherwise, he felt he would have been pressured to provide answers about the thoroughness of any original search of the Rucci's stall. He duly, grabbed two uniformed constables and made his way towards the Market.

As the eleven o'clock London-bound train rattled out of Citadel Station, Armstrong felt ever more confident; his instincts had told him that this murder was little to do with Carlisle. Now, Inspector Standish had found something that could almost prove the theory, if not the identity of the killer. The Cumberland countryside chugged passed the window for ninety minutes before industrial Lancashire thickened around the train.

Inspector Daniel Standish greeted Cornelius with a warm handshake on the platform – the two had attended some training together near Garstang and had developed a healthy respect for each other's work.

In a bothy, off the station platform, not so dissimilar to the one in which Armstrong had interviewed the Platform Supervisor in Carlisle, Standish appraised his opposite number of his findings. A Doctor's Bag had been found hanging in a tree over the River Lune by a couple of boys out playing. What was interesting was that the river runs under a railway bridge; what was even more interesting was the contents of the bag: gloves and makeshift cloth overshoes – both speckled with blood, two heavy stones, and last but by no means least, a large serrated knife. Armstrong took out a magnifying glass from his inside pocket and inspected the knife closely; although it had been wiped, it still bore the remnants of blood and what looked like tiny fragments of flesh under some of the teeth.

"When the bag was brought in, Cornelius," said Standish, "I immediately thought of your message the other day about the possibility of someone on the train. It could be that your man threw the bag from the train intending to find the river, but getting it caught in the overhanging tree instead – he wouldn't have been able to judge things in the dark."

"And the stones were there simply to weigh it down," continued the Carlisle detective to himself. "It's starting to fit together, Daniel. But why would anyone throw the bag out at that point?"

"Well, it's only a couple of miles from Preston," mused Standish, "if he was on the sleeper, he may have been concerned that someone would get on the train and discover the bag. What's more, if he was going to London, this is far enough away to distance himself from it?"

"And far enough from the scene of the murder in the other direction," added Cornelius, nodding.

"Do we know if anyone left the sleeper at Preston, early Sunday morning?"

"I anticipated you asking that and checked with station staff. There is no record of anyone leaving the train that night," said the Preston man.

"This is tremendous, Daniel," said Armstrong shaking hands, "I can't thank you enough."

The whole meeting took little more than twenty minutes and allowed Armstrong to catch the mid afternoon train back to Carlisle. He returned, convinced that he had finally made the breakthrough he had been looking for.

Chapter Nine

The Busy Murder Weapon

"**A**h, this is a Liston Knife, Inspector." An interested Doctor Bell took the knife from Cornelius, who was keen to get the pathologist's view of the weapon. "It was named after surgeon Robert Liston who pioneered its use in limb amputation." The two men sat in the Doctor's office at the Cumberland Infirmary.

"Do you think it could be the murder weapon?" asked the detective.

"Undoubtedly," said Bell, "it is generally accepted that the Whitechapel lunatic used one during his killing spree fifteen years ago."

"It was found in this," said the policeman placing a traditional top-opening doctor's bag on James Bell's desk, "along with some blood-spattered gloves and rags." Armstrong went on to tell the doctor where the bag was found and how it tied in with his theory about the killer's, or killers' escape.

"Well, theories are more your field, Inspector," said the Doctor, "but I can confirm that the wounds on Rucci's body are certainly consistent with the use of a knife like this; and as I told you the other morning, the killer clearly knew how to use the weapon, and on which parts of the body it would cause the maximum damage in the quickest possible time. If he and his accomplice did have a train to catch," added Bell without facetiousness, "the swift use of a weapon like this certainly enabled them to adhere to their tight deadline."

"Could it have been someone with a medical background?" asked Armstrong, pointing to the bag and then the knife.

"Now you are going back to Jack the Ripper conspiracy theories, Inspector."

"I read your postmortem report," said Cornelius, "pretty gruesome."

"It's the nature of the business, Inspector. You can't carve a man up after he's been brutally murdered without it being gruesome."

"*Um* ... well, thank you, Doctor, you've been extremely helpful," said the policeman shaking Dr. Bell's hand, "there is still a long way to go, but this case is finally starting to become a little clearer." Cornelius had little idea that it was to become clearer still, as he caught a Hansom Cab back to the station.

Waiting for him there was Detective Sergeant William Smith. While his superior was following the promising lead to Preston the previous afternoon, Smith was having some success of his own. He and his men had been instructed by Armstrong to carry out a thorough search of Signor Rucci's fruit and vegetable stall at the Market, in the hope that some clue could be found that would shed some light on the brutal killing of his son.

The unoccupied stall had sat unattended since it was covered by a tarpaulin sheet, the day after the murder. Upon pulling back the tarpaulin, there was certainly evidence that the stall had been vacated in a hurry after a long day's work. Scores of pieces of paper – both hand-written chitties, and soft fruit wrappings – littered the floor; several crates had been disturbed and were left where they lay; and even the leftover produce from the busy day was left forlornly rolling around on the cobbled floor.

After twenty minutes of fingertip searching, PC Gibson came across an empty envelope and alerted Smith to his finding – it simply had 'SALVATORE RUCCI' hand-written on the front. It wasn't long before the apparent enclosure was found: under the front of the timber stall, almost hidden

54

beneath some matting that formed the front display, was a screwed up piece of paper that appeared to be written in the same hand. Smith smoothed out the small piece of paper with the side of his hand. The note was brief, intriguing and undoubtedly significant:

> ME AND MARCELLO WANT TO DISCUSS OMERTÀ
> 1 ATKINSON'S COURT
> ★

Smith gave the note to his Inspector upon his return.

"That's old Joe Fargie's house," said Cornelius, almost to himself, as he stared, transfixed at the latest development. "The door to door enquiries on Sunday?" asked Cornelius after some thought, "which houses had no reply?"

Smith rummaged through the bottom draw of his desk, and brought out with a clipboard that contained half a dozen papers; he ran his index finger down the list, "Erm … number seven Annettwell Street … number twenty-three Annettwell, number two Blackfriars Street –" he looked up at his Inspector with ominous realisation, "…and number one Atkinson's Court."

Without waiting to discuss the matter further, and not having removed his hat and coat, Armstrong, turned on his heels and bolted out of the station; Sergeant Smith didn't wait to ask – instead he ordered two uniformed officers to follow the Detective Inspector, who was already running down West Walls towards Atkinson's Court.

Cornelius Armstrong rapped on the door of Joe's house – no reply; he then hammered on the door with the side of his fist. "*Joe? … JOE!?*"

Nothing.

"Break in," he ordered the two constables who had now caught him up.

"Sir?" asked one.

"KICK IT IN MAN, KICK IT IN!" yelled Armstrong, his blood starting to boil.

The two needed no further clarification – after a couple of shoulder charges and kicks with the soles of their boots, the door snapped off its lock and slammed inward against the inside wall.

Inspector Armstrong pushed passed his subordinates and entered the hallway of the old man's home. Despite it being late morning, it was dark and eerily silent. Pausing momentarily to allow his eyes to adjust to the dimness, Cornelius moved forward stealthily towards the open parlour door three or four yards ahead of him. Looking down his heart sank as his saw a trail of dark congealed liquid that had made its way to the threshold of the room - blood. It was then that Armstrong heard a slight whining noise; entering the room his worst fears were realised – it was inevitable.

The fire had long-since burnt out; beside the stone hearth lay Joe's little black pug in its basket. The emaciated dog whimpered, part through hunger and part through shock. He peered over at his master, whose supine body lay two feet away with its throat cut. Armstrong and his men had to cover their noses and mouths as the smell hung in the poorly ventilated room.

The Inspector leaned over the body of his elderly neighbour; whatever muscles the old man had were now gone, and his skin hung about his bones in flaccid sheets. His face was grotesque: only the thinnest layer of flesh was tautly stretched across it so that it gleamed with a curious, blue-white sheen and his eyes seemed sunken back into his head. His stomach bulged slightly and the outline of his ribs could clearly be seen through his shirt. The body was in the early stages of decomposition and had clearly lay there for some time. Cornelius stared in disbelief.

There was something about crimes involving unknown people that allowed the policeman, the lawyer, the doctor to keep the case at an emotional arms length. But this investigation had now encroached into Cornelius Armstrong's space; it had advanced from an exceptional case involving characters from who-knows-where that tested his professional skill and pride, to a very personal case involving a friend and neighbour.

The rich, sickly smell in the room caused by the decaying flesh was stirred up into a dry haze by the draft from the open door and it started to eddy and rise. Armstrong stood transfixed until he inadvertently breathed it in – it flowed into his lungs and burned, and he started to cough. Regaining his composure he ordered one of the men to open the window "… and then make arrangements to have Joe moved up to the morgue. I need to get back to the station." And with a show of affection, Cornelius gathered up the little pug in his arms, "Let's get you out of here, little fella," he said.

He trudged disconsolately along West Walls, knowing full well that he could not have saved Joe, but at the same time, feeling somehow responsible for his death. *God's truth! The whole neighbourhood will be shocked and outraged when this gets out. What next? Protests? Retribution against the Italian community?* The locals saw the young Italian as a slightly distant, unknown figure – Joe was a popular local character. Just when Armstrong thought he was making progress, this had cast an almighty shadow over his investigation and threatened to shatter his reputation.

As he entered the police station, he attracted the attention of Sergeant Townsend on the front desk, who was speaking to someone on the telephone, " … oh, he's just walked in, sir," he said into the mouthpiece. Holding out both hands across the desk, he handed the contraption to his superior officer, "It's Inspector Gregson from Scotland Yard, sir."

Chapter Ten

A Thickening Plot

"I m sorry, Inspector Armstrong," said Tobias Gregson over the crackly line, "I haven't had a moment to call since you wired the other day."

"I appreciate the call anyway," replied the Carlisle detective, "could you just hold the line one moment please?" Armstrong instructed Townsend to get the dog some food and then take it round to Mrs. Wheeler's, where he would attend to it later. "I'm sorry, Inspector, carry on," he then resumed into the mouthpiece.

"You asked in your telegram about an Italian boy?"

"Yes, that's right. I was clutching at straws at the time, but I am pretty sure now there is some connection with London. The young man was called Salvatore Rucci – he was murdered in Carlisle last Saturday night. He moved up here only a few months ago from London to join his parents who came here about twelve months ago. I have reason to believe his killer is from London, as there is evidence he left on the south-bound sleeper minutes after the murder. I understand it's a difficult question to answer but I was wondering if you had ever heard of Rucci?"

There was silence for a few moments before Gregson said, "The name doesn't ring a bell. I must say however, between you and I, Inspector, these Italians are causing all sorts of problems down here too. Gangs of them are fighting each other all over the place over what seem the most trivial of issues. The situation is so bad that murders amongst them are becoming almost commonplace. Only this week, we fished another young fellow out of the Thames."

Armstrong thought back to the books he read about the Mafia and the Camorra. He asked Gregson for his opinion, "Could the murders up here be connected?"

"Murders?" asked Gregson, surprised by the plural.

"Yes, we've just discovered the body of a local man who runs a little boarding house near the station. If my theory about the killer coming on the train is right, it would tally that he stayed at Joe's for a night or two. Left the poor old bugger lying dead for good measure."

"I'm sorry to hear that, but it certainly sounds like some sort of ritual case."

"I wonder if I could beg a favour?" asked Cornelius. "I have a letter written to Rucci a couple of weeks before he died, apparently from a friend of his in Rotherhithe. Could you look this man up and ask him about his connection?" Then referring to the letter, Armstrong read, "His name is Fabio Palletti, he lives at 103 Abbeyfield Road, Rotherhithe."

There was pause that made Armstrong think that the hitherto erratic line had lost its connection completely. "Hello? Are you still there?" he asked uncertainly.

"That's the boy we pulled out of the Thames," said Gregson evenly.

It was now Armstrong's turn to sit in silent disbelief. The day was getting more bizarre by the minute. "How was he killed?" asked Cornelius, eventually.

"He was garrotted," revealed Tobias.

"Well, it seems we have a dual investigation, Inspector," said Armstrong. "There is a clear link between these two lads with the letter from Palletti to Rucci and the fact that they both end up dead by similar methods within a week or so of each other surely proves that they are victims of the same killer."

"I agree," said the Scotland Yarder, "and the more I think about it, the more I believe that they are victims of this stupid family warfare. The boy Palletti had a gang mark on his shoulder."

"What do you mean, a gang mark?"

"Well, each gang has their own mark. As part of their stupid initiations, they tattoo their mark onto a shoulder or a wrist."

Armstrong suddenly remembered Dr. Bell's autopsy report '... *an unconnected raw wound just above the boy's left shoulder blade,*' it had said. "That's it," he said, "Rucci had one too. He must have tried to remove it. These boys were frightened, Gregson."

"With just cause apparently," replied the London Inspector.

The two men knew they would be working together from now on, albeit three hundred miles apart, on their respective element of the murder enquiries. In closing their conversation, they agreed to make regular telephone calls, as soon as one or the other had made progress, in order to keep his colleague up to date.

No sooner had Inspector Armstrong hung the phone up, when Jack Dixon from the *Carlisle Journal* came into the station.

"What's going on, Cornelius?" he asked, "I've just been down to old Joe's – have we got our own Jack the Ripper on the loose?"

"News travels fast," said the Inspector, "and the worse it is, the faster it travels. No we have not got our own Jack the Ripper. You know the process, *Mister* Dixon," Cornelius emphasised the reporter's title, indicating – not for the first time – his displeasure at Dixon's familiarity. "I'll be updating my Chief Constable first on the latest developments, and then we will be releasing a statement."

Dixon wasn't too happy with being fobbed off and started to protest, but a combination of the detective walking away towards his superior's office, and giving a glance to Sergeant Townsend to help the reporter to the door, rendered the newspaper man's protestations futile.

Chief Constable Henry Baker was visibly shocked by Armstrong's revelations: the finding of Joe's body, less than an hour earlier, which ordinarily would have muddied the waters still further; and then his Inspector's telephone conversation with Tobias Gregson that had seemingly unlocked the case.

"What do you propose to do now?" asked the senior officer.

"Well, I think I now know the sequence of events that have taken place to date, but I still don't know the motive, and most importantly, the identity of the killer."

"You are satisfied that it is one man?"

"Almost certainly," said Armstrong. "Foolishly, I thought an accomplice was chasing Rucci, and the boy was running towards the sanctuary of the police station. But in actual fact he received the note young Rose told me about – it wasn't along Dean Tait's Lane and to the left he intended to run, but to the right towards Atkinson's Court. It seems that the killer was staying at Joe Fargie's and was waiting for him at the end of the lane. Covering his tracks included murdering Joe into the bargain. He's then made his escape on the sleeper and fired his bag out of the window before the one and only stop at Preston – if the bag hadn't got caught in the trees I don't think we would have ever discovered his getaway."

After listening intently to the Inspector's account, Baker complimented his friend and subordinate, "I must say, you've excelled yourself this time, Cornelius. You and your theories – where would we be without them?"

"We're not out of the woods yet, Henry. The killer's still at large and if we can follow this through, I think there is a larger criminal ring at work."

"What do you propose?" asked Baker.

Like a festering sore, Armstrong's feelings of unease concerning Salvatore's family – and especially his father – had grown stronger in his mind as the days slipped by since the murder. Now, his feelings were stronger than ever. Years of observation and deduction from given facts could not be swamped by face-saving lies; nor would he allow emotion to deflect him from his search for the truth. "I need to speak with Rucci's father again," he told the Chief Constable.

"Is that wise, Cornelius? We don't want to be accused of badgering the poor people unnecessarily in their grief. It *is* the boy's funeral tomorrow."

"Henry, I can't help feeling that his father knows more than he's letting on. I just need a little bit more time – I'm sure he can help us identify who did this."

"Well, alright, Inspector, but tread very carefully. I don't want this blowing up in our face."

Chapter Eleven

Reflections

Warwick Square consisted of two small independent roads that ran parallel to one another in a southerly direction from one of the city's main thoroughfares – Warwick Road – to the adjacent Aglionby Street at the bottom of each leg of the 'square'. Set between the two roads stood the impressive Our Lady and St Joseph's Catholic Church, with its two entrance gates: one on the corner with Warwick Road and one on west side of the square directly opposite the house of the Ruccis.

Cornelius Armstrong arrived a little after half past six on the dark November evening – just as the pall bearers were removing the coffin from the glass horse-drawn hearse, under the supervision of the top-hatted undertaker. The ominous, muffled church-bell slowly sounded, as if to summon the downcast procession inside, while the glistening black horse restlessly pulled on its reigns and banged its hoof on the cobbles below it.

The Ruccis – like most Italian immigrants – were Roman Catholic. It followed therefore that Salvatore Rucci would receive full recognition in death afforded by the Catholic Church. His body was being carried into church for the Vigil Mass, the night before his burial.

Inspector Armstrong kept a discreet distance while the boy's parents, followed by scores of mourners followed the coffin into church. Many relatives and friends had made the journey to Carlisle and the church was to be near its capacity.

The wind gusted through the bare trees and buffeted the black-clad congregation as they filed through the large doors. It struck Armstrong how odd this dark cold night in the north of England must seem to these people who had emigrated from the idyllic climate of southern Italy. Their faces all bore the same expression: grief and discomfort, mixed with bewilderment and a sense of family duty.

Cornelius, himself, had been baptised and raised a Catholic, due to the influence of his maternal grandparents; how similar, he thought, would be the response of the clannish Irish community in such a circumstance.

When the last of the mourners had disappeared from view, the policeman followed them inside. The poor heating and dimmed lighting in the large church seemed appropriate with the sombre occasion. An elderly church officer with white hair, who appeared to have stewarded many such an occasion was ordering people to the appropriate seats with apparently little sympathy for their emotional state of mind; two considerably younger men were showing a little more compassion to the visitors, whilst at the same time making sure they did not incur the wrath of their senior colleague. Armstrong genuflected and took a rear seat on the north side of the church.

The coffin was placed on its bier in the middle of the church in front of the altar, with the foot of the coffin facing the altar, as was custom with members of the laity. Once everyone had taken their seat, the bell stopped ringing and the church fell into complete silence. Looking at the backs of the mourners, Cornelius could see the juddering shoulders of many women who were clearly sobbing quietly. Something was very wrong about this, he thought to himself – just a feeling gnawing away: *too clannish; too secretive; even a conspiracy of silence.*

At last the door to the sacristy opened and broke the policeman's reverie. Four altar servers holding candles processed in front of the parish deacon, who carried a silver thurible of burning incense, and a tall dark haired priest, vested in the liturgical black. Father Georgio Benedetti had travelled with the young man's maternal grandparents from their home in Glasgow to say the vigil mass and to preside over the funeral the following day. The organist softly played Schubert's *Ave Maria*.

Once on the altar, the deacon wafted the thurible that hung at the end of a long chain; as he fanned it to-and-fro, the ritual urn clicked lightly against its fetter, omitting clouds of incense that billowed out into the congregation before spiraling upwards, towards the high, ornate, timber ceiling of the church.

Finally, the priest commenced the service by chanting in Latin, *"Réquiem, ætérnam dona eis, Dómine; et lux perpétua lúceat eis."*

Armstrong instinctively crossed himself, as did the whole of the congregation. As the hour progressed, Cornelius increasingly found himself gaining some comfort and solace from the service. Perhaps the strain of the week was taking its toll: the murders, the questions, the onus of responsibility. He mused over the lengthy period since he last attended mass and smiled inwardly as he imagined his dear mother's disapproval. By the end of the service, he was pleased he had attended, not just because it afforded him the possibility of unraveling some of the mystery, but it had personally given him some peace of mind.

As the organist played Albinoni's *Adagio,* one-by-one, the congregation fell in behind Salvatore's parents and gradually filed out of church. The detective joined the end of the snake as it made its way across the road to the Rucci's home, presumably for some refreshment. Armstrong knew it was not his place to join them; instead he saw his opportunity to speak with the priest who might be able to give him some objective help in deciphering some of this Italian puzzle.

He made his way back through the eerily silent church, where the incense still hung thick in the air, pausing at the coffin of the young man who had inadvertently started this adventure some days earlier. Knocking on the sacristy door, Cornelius entered to find the participants of the service in a rather less formal demeanor. The altar servers and deacon were putting away the various regalia that had been used during the service, while the priest was hanging up his vestments in a wardrobe at the far end of the room; the elderly church officer was keeping a watching brief, apparently keen to assert his authority, behind the scenes as well as in front of them.

The Inspector addressed the priest, "My apologies, Father but I wonder if I could have a little of your time? I am a policeman – my name is Inspector Cornelius Armstrong and I am investigating the death of Salvatore."

"Certainly," said Father Benedetti, with a friendly smile, "I have been invited over to Rucci's for some supper but a few minutes won't matter, I'm sure." The priest's impeccable English, with a slightly amusing Italian accent, was clearly influenced by his residing in Glasgow for some years. He led Cornelius through a rear door into a corridor that linked the church with the Rectory that stood alongside it. "I'm sure Canon Waterton won't mind us using the front study," he said pointing the way. "Can I get you any refreshment, Inspector?"

"No thank you, Father. I don't want to take up any more of your time than I have to."

"Cornelius Armstrong?" questioned the priest, "that is a very impressive, yet unusual name?"

The policeman smiled, "Yes, a lot of people ask me that. My father's heritage is local – the Armstrongs have been around this area forever! My mother's parents however, moved to Carlisle from Ireland back in 1850 – that's how I got Cornelius. Speaking of moving to Carlisle," he continued, keen to broach the matter at hand, "could I ask you about the case?"

"Of course," said Benedetti sitting down.

"I have reason to believe that young Rucci was somehow followed to Carlisle and murdered by someone belonging to a gang in London. I don't know why it was done, or what the boy had done to deserve it, but it seems as though the killer returned to London on the sleeper train shortly after the murder. For good measure he appears to have murdered the man he was staying with, in Carlisle."

Armstrong took two pieces of paper from his inside pocket. One was the letter from Fabio Palletti to Salvatore; the other was the note found by Sergeant Smith at the Market, apparently written by the killer, and summoning the young man to his death. He laid them out on the table in front of the concerned-looking priest. "I wonder if you could tell me anything about these, Father."

Benedetti studied the notes for a while. Looking up at the policeman, he said, "You are quite correct Inspector. This note here from Palletti is warning his friend that they are both in grave danger."

"And what about this one?" asked Armstrong, indicating the second note, "what does that word mean?" He pointed to the word 'OMERTÀ.'

"It is extremely serious, Inspector," said the Italian, apparently ashamed of some of his countrymen. "It represents a code of silence that forbids members of the Mafia and Camorra gangs from betraying their comrades to the authorities. It is well known amongst Italians that failure to abide by the code can result in death to the individual, or their families." He continued, "See this mark here?" he indicated the multiple asterisks in Palletti's letter and the single asterisk that appeared in the killer's note, "This is the mark of *Il Cinque Punti* – or The Five Points. See the five points of the star?"

It was Armstrong's turn to be ashamed at missing something so obvious. "How can I have been so blind?" he said.

"You could not have known Inspector. They are *Camorristi* from five small towns in the Campania region of Southern Italy who apparently joined together seventy or eighty years ago to do what *Camorristi* do."

"And now they have brought their terrorism here?" Armstrong mused. "I need another favour, Father. It is now all the more important that I speak with Mr. Rucci – I believe he knows more about this. Could you ask him to come here where we could speak in private?"

Chapter Twelve

Revelations

The three men sat in silence in the front study of the Rectory on Warwick Square – the stillness broken only by the ticking grandfather clock that stood in the hallway outside.

It was Armstrong who spoke at last, addressing the boy's father, "Mr. Rucci, do you know Fabio Palletti?"

"Palletti?" repeated Rucci.

"He wrote to your son, shortly before his death," prompted the policeman, "I found his letter when I visited your son's room the other day."

"Ah, *si, si,*" said Rucci, "I don't know him very well. I have heard Salvatore speak of him. They are friends."

"Mr. Rucci, Fabio Palletti is dead," Armstrong said simply. "He was murdered in a similar fashion to your son."

The Italian sunk his head into his hands; he had no tears left to cry – he just sat there, broken.

"I believe that the same people killed both boys. Is there anything you can tell me that will help find them?" asked the Inspector.

Rucci shook his head but did not make eye contact with either the policeman or the priest. Father Benedetti then said something in Italian to his countryman, clearly trying to persuade him to help the Inspector. A few more seconds elapsed before Armstrong exploded.

"*GET A GRIP, MAN!*" he yelled, momentarily forgetting his surroundings. "A local man was also murdered by the

71

man who killed your son," before Rucci had an opportunity to respond, he continued, "How many more people are going to suffer the same fate before something is done?"

Frustrated by the man's intransigence, and having lost most of the sympathy he had previously shown for his loss, Armstrong thrust the two pieces of paper Benedetti had helped him with earlier, in front of the Italian. "Do these mean anything to you?" he asked.

Rucci stared blankly at the notes and absentmindedly rested his forefinger on the symbol of the secret society. Finally, he looked up from one man to the other; completely unprompted, he began to unbutton his overcoat. Without a word, he removed it, followed by his jacket, his waistcoat and finally – to the astonishment of the two men present – his shirt. He then peeled back the left strap of his under-vest and bore his shoulder to the policeman and the priest.

"There," he said, quite lucidly, "There, Inspector. That is what you are looking for. This is the sign of *Il Cinque Punti.*" He pointed to the papers, "It is the same as these here."

"You are a member of this gang?" asked Cornelius, incredulous.

"I was," said Rucci. "Like most young men, I thought I was – how you say?" he turned to Benedetti for help, "*altezzoso –* the priest gave him the translation, "*si, si,* arrogant. I grew up in Montella, one of the five towns that made up *Il Cinque Punti* in Campania. I came to know some bad men who I thought were big and strong and wise. I was a fool! I followed them around like the sheep follows the shepherd. They were *Camorristi* and I became more and more involved in their tricks – robbing, frightening shop-keepers and fighting with other gangs. I even had their mark burned onto me," he added indicating the five pointed star on his shoulder blade.

Armstrong knew this was his opportunity to complete the case; he didn't have to press too hard as the Italian continued his narrative.

"Twenty years ago, I realised there was more to life than the one I had chosen and decided to run away from Italy and *Il Cinque Punti.* I travelled to London but only to find the arm of the *Camorristi* was a long one; there are many Italians in London and many of them are members of the gangs. *Il Cinque Punti* was run by a man called Roberto Busato in Islington, and he wasted no time in finding me and threatening me if I did not help him and his friends with blackmail and violence. He threatened to hurt my beautiful Cecilia who I have met on the ship coming to England." Rucci wept at the thought before regaining his composure.

"Finally, two years ago, I convinced Busato to release me from the gang because of the time I had spent working for them. He allowed it as long as I swore to Omertà. But little did I know that my son had –" looking to the priest again for help with translation "- *inherited* his father's youthful foolishness. I went angry with the boy when he told me he had become part of *Il Cinque Punti* – his friend Fabio as well. I tried to tell him about myself when I was a young man but it did no good. I warned him to be very careful.

"My wife and me came here one year ago to start a new life. We are happy here until Salvatore contacted me to say he needed to come and stay with us. His mother was happy but she did not understand the reason why. I knew there must be something wrong.

"He came in June. When his mother was out I ask him why he comes here. He tells me that he and Fabio have been stealing money from Busato. They frighten shop-keepers to pay money for to protect them and then they give the money to *Il Cinque Punti*. Salvatore and Fabio decide to keep some of the money. *STUPIDO!*" he shouted, thumping his fists on the desk.

He then concluded in quiet contemplation, "I suppose I am the biggest fool of all. I hoped that Salvatore would be safe in this small city, many miles from London. But no, my son is dead."

After the long narrative, Inspector Armstrong spoke, "Mr. Rucci, I would assume that Busato ordered your son's murder, but it is unlikely he carried it out himself. Have you any idea who would have done this?"

To Armstrong's astonishment, Rucci replied simply, "Yes Inspector, I do. Busato always gets the same man to do this work – it is not the first time. His name is John Finch – he is trained in the garratto." Rucci's heavy Italian accent forced him to pronounce the man's name as 'Feench' and he ran his index finger across his neck to illustrate the trade as he did so. "He knows me and has written this letter to Salvatore to bring him from the market and trap him. You see Inspector, I am Marcello, and Finch is suggesting to my son in his note that he is going to kill me because of his betraying the Omertà."

Everything now fitted into place, but Cornelius knew he had an even harder question, "Sir, I have one last thing to ask. In order to bring these men to justice, I will need you to help us find these men and testify against them in court. We will do everything we can to protect you and your wife from harm."

"*Si, si,*" said Rucci, in resignation, "our life is over now. They can't hurt us anymore. I will tell you where they can be found."

Cornelius thanked the two Italians and made his way across the city centre to his lodgings on Abbey Street, where he was delighted to find Mrs. Wheeler and her daughter Emma were taking good care of Joe's little dog. Armstrong was confident that in a few days it would get its strength back. Once inside, he poured himself a glass of rum, picked up the library books that he had referred to earlier in the week and slumped down into his rocking chair by the fire. He leafed through the books until he again found the piece about the gangs of southern Italy and Sicily. There they were, all along, in the text in front of him: *Il Cinque Punti* (The Five Points). "Staring me in the face all the time," he muttered to himself.

But he knew this was a job well done; no longer was he riddled with self-doubt or fear – he had given his Chief Constable and Inspector Gregson of the Yard the answers they were looking for. At some cost however, he thought to himself, recalling the discovery of Joe's body that afternoon and the destroyed lives of Mr. and Mrs. Rucci. Armstrong the historian stared absentmindedly into the crackling fire and thought of Wellington's words after Waterloo, 'There is only one thing worse than a battle won, and that is a battle lost.'

Chapter Thirteen

The Victim

The morning of Saturday 7th November 1903 was fine and mild; a watery autumnal sun took the edge of the sharp temperature.

Salvatore Rucci was just getting used to life in this sleepy backwater his parents had settled in twelve months earlier. It was a little boring for him but in his quieter moments he remembered why he was here and, more importantly, what he had come from – or should that be, who he was running from. The letter he received from his friend Fabio ten days ago had unsettled him a little; Fabio had suggested that Busato and his gang were looking for them both.

Fabio had moved from Islington in the north of the city to Rotherhithe, south of the river, to escape their clutches; he had tried to reassure his friend in the letter that all was well and how he thought that *Il Cinque Punti* would tire of their pursuit, but Salvatore had a little doubt that continued to niggle away at him. In an extreme effort to expunge all traces of the secret society, he had paid a man in the back room of the *Irish Gate Tavern*, to burn off their sign from his shoulder a week ago. His excruciating pain had been the source of much amusement to the group of ruffians who had crowded into the back room to witness the mutilation, but the young man thought it was a pain barrier worth enduring if it helped disguise his identity. Now, a week on, with the wound still tender, Salvatore was preparing for the final day of the week's trading.

Over the past six weeks Marcello Rucci had rather enjoyed the routine he and his son had established, since the latter's unexpected arrival some months earlier. Marcello would now meet the early morning train carrying the fruit and vegetables, organise their transportation to the market, and then be joined by his son during the late morning. Salvatore would then take over the running of the stall, which allowed the Ruccis to stay open until the market closed just before eleven o'clock Monday to Saturday, which in turn led to more profits and less waste.

This Saturday, Salvatore awoke sometime after nine o'clock; an hour later – having hastily consumed the breakfast his mother had made for him – he rushed up to his room, put on his coat and boots and rushed back down again. *"Ciao mama,"* he said, giving his mother a kiss on the cheek. Signora Rucci smiled – contented to have her adoring son back with them again – and told him to have a good day.

By the time Rucci arrived at the Market, it was a hive of activity. The sun beamed through the high glass roof and the clatter of barrows, shuttling back and forth, resonated across the cobbled floor.

His father had enjoyed a steady morning and by early afternoon, Salvatore encouraged him to leave early, full in the knowledge that he had earned his time off. Moreover, the young man was keen to demonstrate to his father that he was willing to knuckle down and assist with the family business. Upon his arrival, some months earlier, Rucci had warned his son that he had not only placed himself in danger by his foolishness, but he had also risked the safety of him and his mother into the bargain. As the weeks had passed, and time had lived up to its billing as a great healer, the boy's father appeared to have come to terms with their predicament and acknowledged his son's efforts to turn over a new leaf. Marcello left around two o'clock telling his son he had a couple of errands to run before going home.

Salvatore passed a relatively quiet afternoon. As produce was sold, he would replenish the front of the stall with fruit and vegetables that stood in pallets in front of the rear canvass sheet; once the pallet was empty, he tossed it to the side of the stall. On the other side of the stall, barrow-boys intermittently loaded their barrows from the same pallets to deliver to customers who had placed orders in writing. Every night, the final task was to move the pallets, sweep the litter from behind his stall and pull the tarpaulin sheet across, in preparation for the following day.

Salvatore was proving to be a popular figure amongst the stall holders and the customers in the Market – his shoulder-length jet black hair, olive skin and big brown eyes gave him an exotic appeal and made him a magnet for most of the female customers. He had struck up a friendship with the beautiful red-headed girl, Rose, who worked at the butcher's stall opposite; but he had to be wary of Rose's employer, Mr. Kelly, who had taken an instant dislike to the boy, and apparently his father.

At around six o'clock, Salvatore saw Kelly leave his stall, presumably to go for something to eat. He couldn't resist crossing the walkway to chat to Rose, who was more than happy to see him come over.

The two chatted for a few minutes before one of the barrow-boys shouted over, "Oi, Sal, are you gonna give uz a hand wid these veggies or wha'?" Salvatore gave a smile of resignation to Rose and, with a shrug of his shoulders, returned to his station to help his charge. As he went to one side of the stall, he didn't see a man approach from the other side.

The remainder of his shift passed relatively slowly; he was sorry to see Mr. Kelly return to his stall shortly after he had helped Jim with his loading; he was even sorrier to see Rose finish her shift half an hour later.

 Finally, at around half past ten, there was the final surge of customers – mainly men who had rolled out of the nearest pub, and who were now hoping to placate their wives by picking up a cheap piece of meat for tomorrow's Sunday dinner. This was the Ruccis' final chance to sell the last of their vegetables that would complete the meal.

Once the crowd had thinned out, Salvatore started to pack everything away; Jim, the barrow-boy had returned from his earlier errand and offered to help. The empty pallets had been assembled on top of each other as the afternoon had worn on, and Jim started to load them onto his barrow, in order to take them to the station in preparation for Monday morning's delivery. As he approached the bottom of the pile, he saw an envelope lying on the cobbled floor under the bottom pallet. Retrieving it he saw it was simply marked 'Salvatore Rucci.'

"Here, Sal," he shouted over, "there's a note here for you."

Young Rucci looked understandably bemused. He opened the envelope and the colour instantly drained from his face. Jim had to support him, as he nearly lost his footing. "What is it?" he asked.

"*Where is this*?" shouted Rucci grabbing at the boy.

Jim looked at the note, "Atkinson's Court? Easiest way is to nip through the Cathedral grounds and then go left along Dean Tait's Lane, then right along West Walls and you're there."

Salvatore dropped the note and shot off out of the main doors, following Jim's directions. Outside, in his haste, he knocked into two women who were standing by an open brazier. Not waiting to see if anyone was hurt, he sprinted up St Mary's Gate, across Castle Street and through the grounds of the Cathedral. His long black hair trailed behind him and his white linen shirt was plastered with sweat against his arms and torso; his heart pounded in his chest as he ran for his life – or that of his father. Running towards the north end of the grounds, he grabbed at the side of the Abbey Gate and created a sling-shot to tear along Dean Tait's Lane, nearly losing his balance in doing so as his leather soled shoes threatened to lose whatever grip they had. Within seconds he was up to full speed again – the lane was a mere thirty yards long and he was almost in sight of his destination. *Nearly there. Keep going.*

"*PAPÀ! PAPÀ!*" he screamed.

He was no more than five yards away from the junction with West Walls, when the end of the lane was filled with a dark figure with an outstretched arm that simply rolled into view from nowhere. Something glinted in the moonlight and a thousand images simultaneously flashed through the young man's mind.

Chapter Fourteen

The Killer

The early morning sunlight shone through the window in John Finch's lodging on Atkinson's Court.

He got up and splashed some water on his face – not long now. Lifting his large carpet bag onto the bed, he took out a smaller doctor's bag. He rummaged through some papers that were inside until he came to what he was looking for: the details of Rucci's whereabouts.

Finch wondered what Rucci's reaction would be and gave a snort of derision. It was only ten days ago that he had found the boy Palletti, trying to hide away, working in the docks. *His face had been a picture. I was the last person he expected to see that afternoon.*

Fabio had never met Finch but he instinctively knew who he was and why he had come. He had written to his friend Salvatore only the day before, expressing his fears for their safety. Now the danger was here. Before the young man could put up a struggle, he had been incapacitated and thrown into a carriage. From there, he was driven to what seemed to be an empty warehouse. Strapped to a chair and heavily beaten, Palletti tried his best to protect his friend by withholding his whereabouts, but he finally gave in to the torture and told Finch that Salvatore was working on his father's market stall in Carlisle. The young man hoped his cooperation would get him a reprieve, but when Finch disappeared from his view, he almost instantly felt the metal band around his neck that gradually tightened and snapped his spinal cord. His body was tossed into the Thames that night.

Finch knew that Rucci's assassination would be considerably more difficult. Timing was everything – too early and he risked being found, and too late would compromise his escape. He decided almost instantly upon his arrival where the best place to kill the boy was; the skill was to lure him there at the appropriate time.

Writing the briefest of notes, he placed it in a pre-marked envelope for Salvatore Rucci. He left his room at four o'clock in the afternoon and descended the stairs; the old man wasn't about so he left, slamming the front door behind him. As he turned out of Atkinson's Court on to West Walls, he saw a uniformed policeman walking away from him about twenty paces ahead. Finch stopped and watched as the patrolman entered the police station a few hundred yards further along. He inwardly castigated himself for not seeing the blue 'Police' sign the previous day. "No matter," he mumbled, "no going back now."

"You alright, mate?" said a voice from behind, "you wanna be careful about talkin' to yourself – they'll carry you away."

Finch turned round to see a man lighting the lamps along the walled lane. Before he had time to say anything, both men instinctively looked across the orchard at the sound of a train rattling its final few hundred yards in towards the station. The lamplighter quipped, "I was down at Liverpool station the other day; I said to the Station Master, *'Is this train going to Speke?'* You know what he replied?...*'Well it's never said anything to me!'* He gave out a staccato laugh.

"Bloody Northerners," snarled Finch under his breath and turned down Dean Tait's Lane, heading towards the Cathedral.

He spent the next couple of hours surveying the area: Paternoster Row and Castle Street; Long Lane and Fisher Street; the Cathedral grounds and St Mary's Gate. *Which was the quickest route? Which was Rucci most likely to take? How long would it take him to reach Atkinson's Court?*

Finch didn't know at this point exactly where the Market was but his exploring of the general vicinity eventually led him to the giant entrance doors on Fisher Street. He entered and found a quiet corner of the bustling trading place, where he could survey the situation and keep an eye out for his quarry. After some time he spotted a sign for 'Rucci's Fruit & Veg.' Sure enough, within a few minutes, a young man dressed simply in a white linen shirt and dark waistcoat appeared from behind the rear tarpaulin sheet. *"Salvatore!"* whispered Finch in triumph. He positioned himself beside an adjacent stall where he could see and hear, whilst he remained unseen and unheard. Salvatore was helping a young boy on the far side of his stall to load some vegetables onto a barrow.

"Where do you want these empty pallets, Sal?" said the youngster, as he emptied the contents onto the barrow.

"Just put them over there on that pile, and we will clear them away later," replied the Italian.

Finch glanced across to where Rucci had indicated to his colleague – three empty pallets stood on the opposite side of the stall to where they were working. The young lad did as he had been instructed. Finch saw his chance: as the two had their backs turned several yards away, he removed the envelope from his inside pocket, and moved swiftly to place it underneath the pile of empty pallets. He turned to leave but caught the eye of a young red-headed girl opposite who was standing watching him. The two held each other's stare for a few seconds before Finch concluded he had to make his escape as quickly as possible.

The murderer knew the next few hours would be tense. *Would Rucci take the bait? When would he come? Will I be able to make my escape in time?* He made his way back to his lodgings, taking the route he believed Rucci would take: through the Cathedral grounds and along Dean Tait's Lane. Once there he let himself in and climbed the stairs to his room. Immediately he knew something was wrong – his bag wasn't where he had left it. Turning his head slowly, his malevolent eyes peered over his shoulder at the closed door. *The old man!*

He carried out a search of his belongings; nothing appeared to be missing, *but what had he seen?* Finch carefully unpacked the doctor's bag and laid the contents on the bed: a few cloth rags, some lengths of string, a pair of gloves and a long serrated knife in a leather sheath. He tied the rags around his feet, creating temporary overshoes; putting on the gloves, he then placed the open doctor's bag inside the larger carpet bag. A final check around the room and it was time.

At the bottom of the stairs, Finch saw old Joe through the open doorway to the front parlour, sitting by the fire. "You've been in my room," said Finch, without ceremony.

"I wasn't poking me nose in, lad," said Joe, "I was just getting the pot under the chair that had your bag on."

"What did you see?" Finch was fired up, not interested in debate.

"I didn't see owt! I wasn't looking for owt!"

Almost before Joe could end his protestations, Finch pulled the old man out of his chair and had him on his tip-toes. It was only now – for the first time proper – that Joe saw his lodger's fearful face: his yellowish wax-like skin glinted in the firelight and the horror instilled by his feral features were exceeded still, by his evil, black, manic eyes. Before Joe had time to protest, struggle or even cry out, the knife was in his neck. His eyes bulged in disbelief as his killer lowered him to the floor. He looked down at the old man – he felt nothing. Joe's little black pug scampered under a table and cowered in terror.

Finch went into the back kitchen and calmly cleaned the blood and pieces of flesh from the knife before placing it back in its sheath. He made himself a cup of tea and a sandwich, while his landlord's corpse lay yards away in the next room.

The seat Finch sat at looked back out into the empty hallway. The hardboard sheets that covered the side of the staircase caught his eye. When he had finished his meal he ripped off a piece of hardboard and held it up against himself – it covered his body from his shins to his neck.

It was approaching eleven o'clock and there was still no sign of Rucci. Finch picked up his bag and the hardboard and closed the front door behind him; he hid in a shadowy corner of Atkinson's Court, waiting and hoping.

Half an hour later and he knew that time was getting very tight. He moved out on to West Walls, concealed himself in a doorway immediately next to the junction with Dean Tait's Lane, and decided to wait there five more minutes before aborting his mission.

Suddenly, he heard the slapping of shoes on the ground indicating someone running; then a yelling that sealed his victim's fate: *"PAPÀ! PAPÀ!"*

The killer silently slipped the knife out of its sheath and rolled around the corner. There was no time for his victim to react or even gasp in surprise; as the young man ran unavoidably at full speed, Finch thrust the long glistening knife into the man's throat.

Time stopped.

The victim stood on tiptoe, held upright only by the knife that protruded through the back of his neck; the gagging body instantly went into involuntarily spasm throughout, like a string marionette dancing for his master. Finally after a few seconds, the body slid almost elegantly from the knife and slumped gently to the floor, spraying blood as it fell. In perfect synchronicity, Finch held up the hardboard sheet to protect himself from any damning evidence.

As soon as the boy hit the ground, the assassin calmly stood the board against the wall, dropped the knife into the open doctor's bag – that sat inside its larger container – and was quickly followed by the cloth overshoes and gloves. Finch then hurried down the steps and through the orchard. He was on the sleeper before the last remnants of blood had drained from his victim's body.

It was over.

Chapter Fifteen

The Toast of London

In all of his thirty-eight years, Detective Inspector Cornelius Armstrong had never been to the nation's capital. The occasional family trip to Silloth in one of the railway outings of the mid eighties, and his detective training classes in Lancashire were almost the sum total of his travelling experiences. He had often envied the military adventures of first, his father, and latterly his cousin, but after resigning himself to the small town existence of a career policeman, he had virtually shelved the idea of travelling and holidays. But now, here he was about to embark on his own adventure: a journey that would finally conclude the infamous Italian Murder case that started five months earlier on that cold November night.

Cornelius settled down into his bunk on the overnight train to London; the irony of this particular journey was not lost on the policeman, as he remembered the night in the pub with George that sparked his original theory concerning the killer's escape. This theory had eventually led to his gaining a confession from Marcello Rucci in the Rectory a week later.

He thought about his neighbour Joe, who inadvertently got caught up in the feud and paid for it with his life, "God love him," he mumbled to himself. The only happy ending involved Joe's little black pug: after several days of nursing the little dog back to health, Cornelius had an idea.

Mrs. Wheeler came up to his rooms and knocked on the door.

"Mr. Armstrong, there is a man down stairs who said you sent for him. Why you would send for *him* is a mystery to me – he's got a face only a mother could love."

"That's alright, Mrs. Wheeler," said Armstrong, with a smile at his housekeeper's observation, "send him up – I'm expecting him."

Moments later, in walked his informant Reuben Hanks.

"Did I hear you say you had lost your dog, the other day, Reuben?"

"That's right, sir," replied Hanks a little sheepishly, "I got tangled up wid ... er ... some characters and ... erm ... I lost me dog!"

Armstrong decided not to pursue the questioning further; instead he picked up the little animal and asked, "How would you like to look after this little bloke then?"

The ruffian couldn't help but be taken with the funny little face of the oriental breed. "What's his name?" he asked.

Cornelius looked at his battered copy of Dumas' *Three Musketeers* that lay open on his desk. "Athos!" he announced.

"*Wha'?*"

"Athos," repeated Cornelius, "he's my favourite literary char ... Never mind, you take him and make sure you look after him."

"Athos," repeated Reuben, picking up the little dog, "yeah, we'll be alright won't we mate?" The two looked approvingly at one another before scuttling off in almost comic synchronicity.

The other loose ends of the case were not so easy to tie up. When Armstrong contacted his fellow Inspector from Scotland Yard, Tobias Gregson, the hunt began for Roberto Busato, the leader of *Il Cinq Punti*, and his hired assassin John Finch. In return for his cooperation, the authorities had agreed to pardon Marcello Rucci for any previous involvement in terrorist activity. Rucci didn't care either way; he was a broken man after his son's murder, and he knew his wife would never forgive him for indirectly influencing their boy in such activity as those carried out by the secret society.

Rucci had given Armstrong as much detail about the ring leader as the policeman could have hoped for, although Armstrong was more interested in the apprehending of Finch than Busato. He knew however that one would lead to the other and his regular feeding of information to Gregson eventually resulted in the apprehension of John Finch in the Dial Square public house in Islington, North London, two days after Christmas. With nothing to lose, and proving the old adage that there is little honour amongst villains, Finch gave Busato's whereabouts to Gregson, who had him arrested before the year was out.

How ironic, thought Cornelius as the train rattled south, that Finch murdered Rucci for threatening to betray Omertà, and yet that is exactly what he did to Busato. Now they were both about to face justice. *No honour amongst thieves or garrotters, I suppose.*

Inspector Gregson was at King's Cross Station with a four-wheeler, to greet his opposite number from Carlisle. The two had looked forward to meeting one another for many months, and neither was disappointed when they met. Gregson in particular was fulsome in his praise of Armstrong's work. "I have to say, Cornelius," he said as they drove across London towards the Central Criminal Court, "I can't thank you enough for the work you have done on this case. I can't help feeling it is we Scotland Yarders who are getting all the credit, and all we seemed to do was pick these ne'er-do-wells up. It was all your groundwork that solved the murders."

"Well, the main thing is that between us, we managed to apprehend them," Armstrong replied modestly. "Hopefully they will now get their comeuppance." He was only half listening to Gregson as he stared out of the window in wonderment at the stunning architecture of central London. One of his favourite paintings – a print of which hung on his sitting room wall above his piano – was Canaletto's depiction of the Thames and St Paul's Cathedral on Lord Mayor's Day in 1747. Now here he was seeing the landmarks for himself for the first time, along with the Palace of Westminster and the Old Bailey itself.

Stepping down from the carriage on the steps of the courtrooms, the Carlisle man snapped out his daze, as the magnitude of the case suddenly dawned on him; Rucci's murder was certainly a big story in his home city, but the ring of villainy it had uncovered had projected the case onto the national stage. As he entered the building, he thought about some of the famous and infamous characters that had trodden this path over the years.

Once inside the ante-room of Number One Court however, Armstrong the tourist, Armstrong the historian, became Armstrong the Police Inspector again. The trial was in its second day and it was the Carlisle policeman's turn to give evidence; at eleven o'clock he was called.

He entered the large courtroom, with its ornate decor and its head-height oak paneling throughout. Cornelius felt like a small boy as he walked the length of the room under the gaze of scores of people above him: the public in the gallery, the opposing counsels in their wigs and gowns, and the imposing judge, Sir Anthony St John-Brown, who watched the policeman's every step from over the top of a pair of glasses that hung precariously from the edge of his nose.

It was only when Inspector Armstrong climbed the few steps into the witness box that he could look up to the dock and see the man he had been tracking. Finch did not return his pursuer's gaze; instead he looked straight ahead, his smooth, wrinkleless face giving nothing away. Standing beside him was a squat swarthy character – presumably Busato. Beside him were a number of associates, who had all been implicated in the crimes of *Il Cinq Punti;* one of the men worked as a railway official and he was charged with aiding and abetting Finch by organising his journeys to and from Carlisle under a pseudonym.

Armstrong spent two hours giving evidence in the trial; he took the court through the sequence of events starting with the discovery of young Rucci's body, to the point where Inspector Gregson telephoned him on New Year's Eve to inform him that Busato and his gang were all in custody.

Marcello Rucci had given his evidence the previous day and was not in court to see the policeman articulate his investigation. Cornelius took his seat in court alongside Inspector Gregson, once he had fulfilled his duty as a witness for the prosecution. The jury retired later that afternoon to consider their verdict; it was thought that their deliberation would take them into the following day – given the lateness of the hour – but less than fifty minutes had elapsed when it was indicated that a verdict had been reached. Armstrong was concerned about the briefness of the jury's considerations, almost convincing himself that the long invisible yet influential arm of *Il Cinq Punti* had reached into the jury room.

His concerns were quickly erased: "Guilty," stated the foreman when asked about Finch's murder charge; "Guilty," he repeated concerning Busato's conspiracy to commit murder. Ten minutes later, the foreman was still repeating the decision of his colleagues, each time with more gusto, when asked about the seemingly endless charges of embezzlement, blackmail and kidnap. Murmurs of approval came from the public gallery – Armstrong assumed that many there had been victims of Busato's evil operation.

Finally, the judge reached for the black cap, which he placed on top of his long wig and addressed the two primary defendants. "You are evil men who would apparently stop at nothing to further your own gain. Had it not been for the work of Inspector Gregson of Scotland Yard, and especially of the investigation carried out by Inspector Armstrong of the Cumberland Constabulary, your nefarious activity may never have been uncovered.

"After years of apparently evading the law, you have now been found guilty of the murders of Fabio Palletti in London, and Salvatore Rucci and Joseph Ferguson in Carlisle, in the county of Cumberland, during October and November of last year. For these crimes, you will be taken from this place and hung by the neck until you are dead. Take them away." The remaining defendants were given various sentences including hard labour and deportation.

Armstrong and Gregson allowed themselves a congratulatory handshake as the convicted men were led away. That night, the London detective provided accommodation for his provincial colleague after treating him to a meal at Marcini's, one of London's finest restaurants.

The following morning, Armstrong bought a copy of *The Times* from a news-vendor outside the station. Settling into his seat to commence his long journey home, he read with pride about the trial and his part in the case. The editor detailed the judge's comments about the Carlisle man and expressed his paper's thanks '...on behalf of many of the capital's citizens, by putting an end to one of the most violent Italian gangs to terrorise the streets of London.'

King Edward's Ghost

Chapter One

Christmas Eve, 1906

It was a bitterly cold evening, which came as a shock to the people of Carlisle. They had enjoyed an unseasonably mild December but, as if sensing the occasion, and its role in the imminent festivities, the temperature plummeted, the fog descended and frost was already appearing on the pavements around the Cathedral, making it difficult for the midnight worshipers who were due to gather in a few hours time. Half a dozen young carol singers were grouped around a quartet of Salvation Army bandsmen on Paternoster Row as they softly played *The First Noel;* their faces lighted by the rays of a horn lantern carried by the tallest of the group.

Further along the Row, on the corner with Abbey Street, a group of men – waiting for *The Board* to open – stood around an open brazier to the side of the Abbey Gate. But no amount of hand-rubbing and foot-stamping could combat the wintry chill; their faces crimson; their eyes watery. Looking down the street, they could see the rear of a hansom cab, silhouetted against the soft lights of the gas lamps, as it stood patiently outside number 22a, waiting for its fare. The cabby was muffled to the eyeballs in his winter wear but, nothing succeeded in keeping out the cold on such a night as this. His breath was visible as it rose into the dark sky; his horse pulled on its reign and banged its hooves on the cobbles, as if keen to get on with its journey.

Inside 22a Abbey Street, Cornelius Armstrong stood in front of the mirror straightening his white tie. He was immaculately dressed in his black, tailed coat, matching trousers and patent leather shoes. A beautiful pearl pin held his collar in place and his starched cuffs – which protruded from the sleeves of his coat – were fastened with matching studs.

He was preparing for the annual Christmas merrymaking of his superior, Chief Constable Henry Baker, at his spacious villa, across the river in Etterby Village. The two had been friends and colleagues for almost twenty years, and Cornelius was one of the few guests to be invited every year. Rather than having the same people year after year, Baker preferred to invite a diverse mix of local dignitaries and associates. This year, Armstrong noted, the guests included Mr. Robert Slater, manager of the Green Room Theatre on West Walls, Geoffrey Howard, the newly elected Liberal MP, and the Reverend Edmund Hope from St Cuthbert's Church, and his colleague, the recently arrived, Reverend Richard Fraser, from St Michael's Church at Burgh by Sands.

As the policeman stood there, giving the horns of his moustache a final twist, there was a light knock on the door and in came his housekeeper Mrs. Wheeler carrying a large box that was decorated with a red ribbon. "I knew you'd be getting dressed in all your finery, Mr. Armstrong," she said, "so I couldn't resist bringing you your Christmas present a few hours early."

Cornelius opened the box: inside was a black Homburg hat, "Oh, Mrs. Wheeler, this is beautiful!" he cried, giving her a hug, "Merry Christmas. And thank you, you shouldn't have gone to so much expense."

"It's only once a year," replied Mrs. Wheeler, "you enjoy your evening, sir."

Cornelius put on his new hat and admired himself in the mirror; he levered himself into his black overcoat, wrapped himself with his long woollen scarf, put on his leather gloves and left to meet his cab downstairs.

"Cold enough for you, sir?" asked the cabby, as the policeman climbed in.

"Certainly is, John" affirmed Cornelius, 'quick as you like,' he added, referring to the forthcoming journey.

Upon his arrival he was welcomed at the door with a kiss from Baker's wife, "Hello, Cornelius, it's lovely to see you again."

"And you, Mary. You look lovely as ever, if you don't mind me saying."

Inside, he discovered he was virtually the last to arrive: the large reception room was filled with gentlemen in their dark evening wear, and ladies in their brightly coloured dresses, sipping sherry and engaging in polite conversation about the weather and the Liberal Reforms – something the recently elected Geoffrey Howard was championing with anyone who was prepared to listen. Cornelius was introduced to a handful of the guests before they were called in for dinner.

At the dinner table, he found himself seated between Mrs. Slater, the wife of the theatre manager, and Reverend Richard Fraser from St Michael's at Burgh. Fraser was the archetypal churchman: bespectacled in his early fifties, with rather unkempt graying hair and a permanent smile. As the soup was being served, it was he who started the conversation, "And what is life like for a Detective Inspector, Detective Inspector?" he asked, amused by his own cleverness.

"Oh, fairly mundane, really," answered Armstrong modestly.

"Don't listen to him!" interrupted Henry Baker from the head of the table, "he is the best policeman this city's got. If there is ever a problematic case that comes our way, Cornelius is always the first man I turn to."

"I have heard as much from Edmund, at St Cuthbert's," said the clergyman indicating towards his colleague further down the table, who was engrossed in a separate conversation with his dining neighbour, "he has told me about many of your cases."

"Well, it's very kind, I'm sure," replied Cornelius, slightly embarrassed, "but the press do tend to embellish some of the stories. Thankfully, here in Carlisle, we don't have some of the problems other larger towns and cities have." Keen to move the conversation away from his own exploits, Armstrong quickly changed the subject. "So how are you finding life at Burgh, Reverend?"

"Call me Richard, please," replied the clergyman with a smile. "I'm settling in nicely thank you; I've been there around four months now, I think. The locals seem very friendly and I know Edmund –" he pointed again to his colleague "- and the Reverend Nicholas Stuart from the Cathedral, so all in all, I'm enjoying my time immensely."

"Reverend Hope is lovely, isn't he?" said Mrs. Slater, "my husband and I go to St Cuthbert's every Sunday. He is a great story-teller; his sermons are most enjoyable."

"Yes, he is an inspirational figure," agreed Reverend Fraser.

"Are you a churchgoer, Inspector," asked Mrs. Slater of Cornelius.

"Not as often as I should be, I must confess," said the policeman. "I was christened a Roman Catholic – my mother's family came over from Ireland in the '50s – but I consider myself a Christian first and a Catholic second. Tomorrow for example, I intend to go along to the service at the Cathedral to celebrate Christmas."

"Well said, that man!" said Richard Fraser, "there is only one relationship that matters: the one between you and God. No one else is important and no one else has the right to influence you one way or another."

As the various desultory conversations around the dinner table continued and the noise level grew, Mrs. Slater asked Cornelius, "So will you be getting time off over the holidays?"

"Yes, although I don't have a great deal of domestic commitments, so I'll be popping into the station now and then to keep an eye on things from time to time."

"And how does an off-duty policeman fill his time?" asked Fraser.

"Well, I do a lot of reading, I play the piano – very poorly, I might add – and I like to get out walking and do a little bird watching."

"Really?" exclaimed the vicar, "I love to do a little bird watching myself. I have found there is nothing better than to get out on to the marsh on a winter's afternoon, with your field glasses. I'm actually a member of the King Edward Ghost Hunters," he said with a laugh.

"The King Edward Ghost Hunters?" repeated Cornelius, joining in the joke.

"Yes – I wasn't in the parish very long before I met up with two or three like-minded locals – avid bird watchers like myself. We can be regularly seen wandering out on to Burgh Marsh. Some wag in the pub claimed we were hunting for the late King's ghost, and the name stuck, much to everyone's amusement."

"The late King?" quipped Armstrong, "He's not dead is he?"

"Not the Seventh, Inspector, the First," replied the vicar, not getting the joke.

"Ah, I see," said Armstrong politely, whilst inwardly cringing.

"Things have developed further after I suggested we start a study group to look at the life of Edward – something to promote the community spirit," added the vicar. "There are now almost a dozen locals who gather in the pub on the first Saturday afternoon of the month to share their findings and toast 'absent friends'."

"Sounds interesting," said Cornelius, "I'm an amateur historian myself."

"Why, we have so much in common, my dear Inspector," replied Fraser, "why don't you come and join us over the holidays?"

"Well, we'll see," said Cornelius, with an uncommitted tone.

"Yes you must," persisted the vicar, "there is a veritable cornucopia of species on the marsh: herons, swans, gulls, terns, and any number of waders. We could then retire to the local hostelry and discuss the life of old 'Longshanks'. I'm sure my fellow ghost hunters will be delighted with your company."

"Ghosts?" questioned Baker from down the table, "who mentioned ghosts?"

The Reverend Fraser repeated his story to the rest of the guests who had now all stopped and turned at their host's exclamation.

"It's quite timely that you should mention King Edward's ghost, Richard," said his fellow clergyman from St Cuthbert's, who had been in the Diocese for many years, "he should be coming out to play shortly."

"I'm not sure I understand you, Edmund," replied Fraser.

"Well there is an old wives tale isn't there that every one hundred years, the ghost of the King can be seen on and around the marsh. As we are moving towards 1907, I make it six hundred years exactly since the old boy breathed his last. He must therefore be due for a bit of an airing!"

"Poppycock!" exclaimed Fraser with a laugh, "I never heard such a thing."

"Yes," persisted the Reverend Hope, "something about him looking for one of his courtiers? Maybe you could make it the subject of your next study group meeting."

Much to everyone's amusement, further banter continued between the two clergymen; all of which gave the host for the evening an idea.

Chapter Two

Fireside Ghost Stories

As snow started to fall outside, Henry Baker, instructed his staff to clear away the table, ensure the glasses of his guests were re-filled, and then invited them to gather round the crackling fire. As the general conversation amongst his guests had turned towards phantoms and the paranormal, he announced, "What better way to round off the evening than with some Christmas ghost stories!"

Like the Reverend Hope, Baker was a great storyteller himself, and, in keeping with the time of year, the two proceeded to entertain their companions with anecdotes of various ghostly stories and sightings – some from classic literature, and some a little closer to home: atmospheric tales of foggy moors, and dark cavernous houses with creaking doors and mysterious occupants. The clergyman narrated a story from the master of the ghostly tale, Henry James, while the senior policeman followed it with a rendition of Mr. Poe's sinister beady-eyed raven.

As the clock ticked towards midnight and the blazing logs burned evenly in the grate, the suspense grew amongst his guests, and Baker decided to deliver his *coup de grace*: his reciting of the ghost of a Black Friar in the West Walls area of Carlisle. Adopting the classic velvety tone of the skilled storyteller, he told how the Black Friars came to Carlisle in the thirteenth century and established their permanent site on the street that is now named after them.

With his guests transfixed, he continued "... These were dangerous times for the city and its inhabitants and when it was attacked by Scottish forces, a group of Black Friars were thought to be stranded near the castle. The marauders were known to have little sympathy for the religious order and one of the Friars, locked safely in the Convent, was so concerned about his brothers he insisted on going out to look for them. His fellow-priests begged him not to go – it was a foul night – dark and stormy – but the warnings went unheeded. The Friar was inevitably captured and tortured to death by having his eyes burned out with a hot poker. The tragedy was that his colleagues had found their way back to the Convent by using an underground passageway that led to an old vaulted chamber that lay under the building. The spirit of their poor brother is said to roam around West Walls to this day, reaching out for his colleagues."

With his wide-eyed guests gripped by the story and hanging on his every work, the story-teller moved towards his grand finale. "I will give you this piece of advice: if you are unfortunate enough to encounter the apparition, never look into the black eye sockets of the blinded wretch, for…"

Just then, the spell was broken when a log collapsed in the grate, causing more than one of the ladies present to jump, much to the amusement of everyone else.

"Knowing you, Henry," said Cornelius, addressing his superior colleague, "I swear you arranged for that log to collapse at that very moment, for effect."

"You know me so well Cornelius," replied Baker with a smile and a wave of the hand, "ever the showman." He looked at his dear wife; she simply rolled her eyes and tossed her head back in mock disapproval, having seen and heard it all before.

"Do you believe in ghosts, Inspector?" asked Mrs. Slater as the room re-gained its composure.

The question attracted the attention of many, and much to Cornelius's embarrassment, most of the guests turned to hear his answer.

"Well, as a matter of fact I do," he said at last. Armstrong sensed the reaction to this revelation was mixed so decided to explain his thoughts. "I'm not sure how my clergymen friends will view my views but I believe that some people, when they die, fail to get across to the other side."

Mrs. Slater gave an uncomfortable laugh, "I don't understand," she said.

"I knew someone once who was a soul-saver," he continued in response to Mrs. Slater's questioning expression, "he had a gift that he claimed allowed him to see the spirits of those who had died unexpectedly; he would then try and help them to get over to the other side. I must confess he convinced me about the existence of spirits on earth."

"Unexpectedly?" questioned his fellow guest.

"When we move towards death," explained Cornelius, "I believe that the body and the mind prepare themselves; so when the moment comes, our spirit moves towards the light because it knows the time is right and it is at peace. If, on the other hand, say, someone is murdered or dies in an accident – 'before their time' – as some older folk might say, then their spirit goes into shock and is frightened by the approaching light. They do not go through, and over to the other side, therefore, leaving their confused ghostly forms to wander around the place of their death."

"Why can't everyone see them, then," asked Mrs. Slater's skeptical husband, who had been drawn in by the policeman's vehemence on the subject.

Cornelius had been less than impressed by the theatre manager – earlier on in the evening, he overheard him talking to his dining partner in hushed tones and referring to the clergymen present as 'gospel wallopers'. He replied politely but firmly.

"Many don't share such a belief and therefore can't see them or don't bother looking."

"And how can you justify such a stance when you spoke earlier about your religious beliefs?" asked Slater mischievously, knowing that the Reverend Fraser was listening to the conversation.

"I don't think such a belief compromises my faith at all," replied Armstrong with some confidence. "By suggesting spirits exist doesn't mean that God and heaven don't. On the contrary, I think it supports Christians' belief that there is life after this."'

"Well said that man," said Richard Fraser, leaving the theatre manager feeling a little chastened. "We should not fall into the trap of simply conforming to man's arrogant assumptions. As Christians we believe the spirit lives on after death, so it is not inconceivable that there are spiritual forces here on earth. After all we all acknowledge that there are great mysteries regarding our faith; as long as you are at peace with your conscience, and you don't give way to harmful delusions or open your heart to malevolent forces, then your belief system is simply between yourself and your God."

Mrs. Slater sensed a slight tension developing in the conversation and attempted to lighten the mood somewhat. "Have you seen any ghosts yourself?" she asked Cornelius.

"None that I am aware of," replied Armstrong with a smile, acknowledging the attempt of his fellow guest to defuse a potentially uncomfortable situation, "but we should always be ready, for we know not when the day will come!" Everyone laughed and the conversation moved on in desultory fashion.

The evening gradually drew towards its conclusion and by the time the various modes of transport had arrived at the Bakers' villa to ferry their guests home, the snow was thickening. It was shortly before one o'clock in the morning when they started to don their coats and scarves, and amid numerous handshakes, kisses and wishing each other 'Merry Christmas', they dispersed into the night.

As Reverend Fraser and Cornelius Armstrong thanked each other for their company and wished each other well, the former said, "I will be in touch, Cornelius, about your visit."

Armstrong was a little unsure how to respond, as he did not know how serious Fraser's original offer was. Rather than labour the issue, he decided to see how it developed, wished his companion well and climbed into the hansom.

The relatively short journey back to Abbey Street took twenty minutes, as Cornelius's driver picked his way carefully along the slippery tracks and cobbled streets that were icing up as the temperature dropped still further. Cornelius looked out of the window at the Carlisle skyline across the river, as his cab started its decent down the steep bank towards the Eden Bridges; the city's roof-tops were already capped in snow.

Safely back in Abbey Street, the detective paid his fare and added a substantial tip for the cabbie's inconvenience on such a night. "Compliments of the season to you and your family, John," he said with a handshake.

"And the same to you, Mr. Armstrong, sir," replied the driver, tipping the brim of his hat.

As Cornelius put the key in the door, his eye fell on the knocker and he stopped for a moment, thinking of the ghostly nature of the conversation during the latter part of the evening. He waited to see if the lion's head – from whose mouth hung a heavy cast iron ring – was going to turn into the spectre of an old acquaintance, as it had once done for Mr. Dickens's Ebenezer Scrooge on a Christmas Eve long since past. A few moments later Cornelius smiled to himself and, after concluding there would be no phantoms tonight, went inside.

Chapter Three

The Invitation

The Cathedral bells rang out for joy as a new Christmas morning was celebrated. Cornelius Armstrong drew back the curtains and discovered the snow had continued to fall heavily throughout the night, leaving Abbey Street – and presumably the rest of the city – snow-capped and ice-bound. Across the street, in the rear gardens of Tullie House, the trees sagged under the excess weight, while confused birds hopped over the white covering, in their futile search for food.

Within the hour – and as he had suggested the previous night – Cornelius's footfall made a crunching sound as he waded through the snow along Abbey Street to attend the morning service. Walking through the Abbey Gate, the Cathedral grounds made a beautiful winter scene. The bells continued to summon the townsfolk to worship; Cornelius watched them and smiled as they waddled uncertainly in single file along the slippery, compacted walkway towards the main door, like a long file of penguins leaving their colony.

Many of them – Armstrong included – did not grace the church on a regular basis, but making that once-a-year visit to the morning service was as traditional as the Christmas pudding they would enjoy later in the day. This fact did not seem lost on one church warden who had apparently been detailed to welcome the congregation – a task he was clearly unsuited to. Living and working in the area, and regularly walking through the cathedral grounds, Cornelius vaguely recognised the man as being one of the many cathedral personnel that could be seen moving between the many buildings in the grounds that were collectively known as the Abbey. Despite Inspector Armstrong's standing in the neighborhood, the man did not seem to – or perhaps chose not to – recognise the policeman at all.

"Merry Christmas," said Cornelius to the man with a smile, as he followed in a young couple and their three children through the main doors. The tall wiry figure had a high forehead and a long nose, down which he looked at the individual before him, as if he was being asked for money.

"And to you, I'm sure," he said haughtily, indicating with his arm that people should keep moving along.

"Full of Christmas cheer," said Armstrong to the father of the young family.

The young man replied with a nod and a look of antipathy, "And Christian spirit," he agreed, just loud enough for the man to hear him.

Notwithstanding the unnecessary and objectionable experience at the cathedral door, Cornelius enjoyed the morning service immensely. As the choir led the final carol *Hark the Herald Angels Sing,* it triggered thoughts of his childhood: singing and playing at Sunday school, and Christmas carols in the streets where he had first heard some of the hymns sung this morning.

Before returning home, and with all childhood memories squirreled away, it was then time for a very adult past-time. He walked the short distance to *The Board* on the corner of Paternoster Row and Castle Street, where another tradition dictated that he met up with his cousin George for a Christmas Day lunchtime drink. Sergeant George Armstrong of the Border Regiment had enjoyed a quiet few years based at the depot in Carlisle, after returning from the war in South Africa. He was now due to be posted out to India with the Regiment and both cousins knew this would be the last such drink they would enjoy for a year or two. Cornelius enjoyed the company of his cousin and best friend for a couple of hours.

It was then back to his lodgings. In the years that he had been lodging with the Wheelers, it had become a tradition for Cornelius to accept their kind invitation of having Christmas dinner with them in their dining room on the ground floor. He always responded by purchasing a bottle of fine claret for the table.

As Mr. Wheeler carved the traditional festive bird, Cornelius poured everyone a glass, including young Emma who received a consensual nod from her father as Armstrong held the bottle over her glass awaiting permission to pour.

"And now, ladies and gentlemen," said the policeman, "a toast: to good food, and good friends, God Bless us all and a Merry Christmas."

"Hear, hear!" they collectively cried.

As always, Isabella Wheeler did her family and lodger proud with a fine goose and a delicious Christmas pudding.

While the Wheelers spent the rest of the day visiting Isabella's sister in Wapping, Cornelius retired to his rooms and enjoyed his own company. Thankfully for the off-duty policeman, the remainder of the Christmas week was as quiet as that peaceful afternoon. The station was close enough for him to pop in to see if anything was amiss, but much of the week was spent either at home reading and playing the piano, or walking and bird-watching in the park behind the castle.

It was three days after Christmas when a stunningly crisp morning drew Cornelius out for one such walk. Under the Eden Bridge and following the footpath along the river, down to where it is joined by the Petteril at Stoney Holme, on such a beautiful and tranquil morning proved an exhilarating experience; then back up the other side and through the park with the rear of the castle across the open ground to his left. The solitary figure paused and looked through the skeletal trees and across the white field at the giant red structure that was silhouetted against a low winter sun. *A stunning sight,* he thought to himself – one he never tired of.

Suddenly, a flash of colour caught his eye down by the river bank – a kingfisher. Cornelius reached in his inside jacket pocket for his miniature telescope. He watched through the lens for a few minutes until the bird took to flight, following the line of the river until it disappeared from sight. The off-duty policeman pushed the brass tubes back together with a snap and smiled to himself. *A perfect end to a perfect morning.*

He arrived back at Abbey Street with a hearty appetite shortly after noon. Mrs. Wheeler was waiting for her lodger, not only with another fulsome meal, but with some unexpected news.

"There was a letter arrived for you Mr. Armstrong," she said as he entered. "Cem about an hour ago."

It was certainly unusual for the policeman to receive a letter at home; given his close proximity to the station, any emergencies normally resulted in a uniformed officer coming to call, and with no family or friends living away from Carlisle, there was never any instance of the postman needing to deliver personal information. It was with great curiosity therefore that Cornelius ripped open the message and smiled.

My Dear Cornelius

Thank you once again for your entertaining company on Christmas Eve at the Bakers' party. I am writing to repeat my invitation for you to come out and visit us here in Burgh. As I live on my own in the vicarage, I have plenty of room - why don't you stay for a day or two? I also have one of those new-fangled telephones in the vicarage (whatever next?). Give me a call and we can make some arrangements.

Look forward to hearing from you soon.

God Bless

Richard Fraser

"Everything alright Mr. Armstrong?" asked his housekeeper.

"Yes, everything's fine Mrs. Wheeler. It's from a gentleman I met at Mr. Baker's party the other night – he's the new vicar at St. Michael's Church at Burgh-by-Sands. He invited me over to visit and do some bird watching with him and his friends." Cornelius had almost forgotten about the casual offer. "He's been as good as his word," he concluded holding the telegram in the air.

"Will you be going then sir?" asked Isabella, "It'll be a nice change if you ask me."

"I don't know, I hadn't really thought about it. He says he has a telephone at the vicarage – I will give him a call later."

Armstrong pondered Reverend Fraser's offer over lunch; he was the archetypal home-bird, never straying far from his rooms, even during time away from work. But he did acknowledge that Burgh would provide a change of scene and the opportunity to see some of the birds on the marsh would be very different from those he regularly watched in the parklands of the city. So by the time he had walked the few hundred yards to the station to use the telephone, his mind was virtually made up.

The operator connected him and the unmistakably jovial voice of the clergyman crackled over the line.

"My dear Cornelius, how wonderful to hear from you!"

'Hello, Richard. I received your letter this morning."

"So you are coming out then?"

"I couldn't possibly refuse after you've gone to so much trouble," said the detective.

"Splendid, splendid!" cried the Reverend, "'When can you come?"

"Well, I do have a few things to sort out, so I think it would have to be New Year's Day." Armstrong then paused, "Oh, wait a minute, there won't be any trains running on New Year's Day," he said.

"No matter," said Richard, "I could send Mrs. Hunter's husband into town to collect you."

"I don't want to put anyone to any unnecessary trouble. How about if I walk up to Kirkandrews-on-Eden and he can pick me up there? I will enjoy the walk."

"An excellent idea! I will tell Hunter; shall we say around eleven o'clock?"

"That will be fine, Richard. I will look forward to seeing you on Tuesday."

The next few days passed in much the same fashion as the previous few. While the sounds of revellers, enjoying the final night of the year, filtered up from Abbey Street below, Cornelius Armstrong packed some effects into a rug-sack for the following day's adventure.

Chapter Four

A New Year Break

Carlisle woke up to a bright and clear New Year's Day 1907. As Cornelius set out on his journey around half past eight, he marveled at the blue sky broken only by a beautiful pale film of moon. At a quarter to eleven he found he had made good time and was sitting in the tiny hamlet of Kirkandrews-on-Eden waiting to be picked up, as discussed with Reverend Fraser.

He had scarcely halted for five minutes when there rattled into view a rather worn and tattered pony and cart. The mottled animal was predominantly light brown; a small, shaggy-looking creature that wore blinkers; its driver was a ruddy-cheeked middle aged man with a large cap pulled down over his brow. As he drew up to the solitary figure standing by the road, he removed it.

"Mr. Armstrong, sir?" he asked cordially.

"Yes," replied Cornelius, "you must be Mr. Hunter; it's very kind of you to come and meet me."

"No problem, sir. Call me Sam," said Hunter making room on the bench of his wagonette, and indicating his passenger throw his rug-sack in the rear. Cornelius climbed aboard and Sam maneuvered his cart round. With a double click of his tongue and a deft slap of the reigns, the small pony responded to his master's encouragement: the rickety old wagonette lurched into motion and they were on their way.

The morning may have started bright and clear but as the tiny vehicle meandered its way over the rough track to Burgh, the sky had become almost silver. The only sounds Cornelius could hear above the trotting of the pony's hooves and the creek of the cart were the harsh cries of gulls from near and far. Hunter skillfully guided the small animal over the rough bumpy track with a firm but gentle hand until they came into sight of the village: an eclectic mix of cabins, functional thatched cottages and detached villas with their elegant gables and mullioned windows. There was a rough scraping of the wheels as the cart pulled up on the stones outside St Michael's Church.

"The Reverend said he had an errand to run, sir," said Hunter as his passenger climbed down from the wagonette. "He said he would be along as soon as he could. Hopefully, I will see you later on, when I come to pick the missus up."

"Thank you again, Sam for your kindness," said Armstrong with a handshake.

He watched as the rickety vehicle pulled off and then turned his attention to the church. Full of character, its scarred stones, battered by the wind, were said to have been taken from Hadrian's Wall when the church was constructed on the site of the Roman fort of Aballava, in the twelfth century.

Two overhanging yew trees framed a wrought-iron gate; the lever clanked up and the gate opened with a rusty squeal. Within the churchyard, on either side of the path, stood around fifty old gravestones. Many of them were lodged at drunken angles and almost all were covered in patches of greenish-yellow lichen and moss, scoured pale by the salt wind, and stained by years of driven rain; virtually no names or dates were decipherable. The neglected plots had been conquered by weeds and nettles. "How soon the dead are forgotten," Cornelius mumbled to himself.

Peeping out from behind the church was a building he took to be the Old Vicarage with the infamous Burgh Marsh beyond it – King Edward's Monument could just be made out in the distance. But it was towards the church porch Armstrong found himself being drawn. He paused in the covered entrance before trying the large wooden door. He was somehow surprised to find it unlocked. With a feeling of slight unease, Armstrong entered the church; all was still and dark.

He was unaware of any other presence until, with a slight start, he saw a parishioner at the far side of the third pew from the front; whoever it was, they were kneeling with their head bowed in prayer. The figure appeared to be wearing a dark red coat but Armstrong couldn't make out whether it was a man or a woman. He didn't want to disturb them unnecessarily and opted instead to keep his distance. After a while of admiring the interior of the church, he became increasingly uncomfortable and aware of a presence close by. He slowly turned to behold a figure appearing from the darkness.

"Reverend Fraser!" he exclaimed, surprised by his own feelings of anxiety.

"Inspector," enthused the vicar with a hearty handshake, "how wonderful to see you again. I'm delighted to welcome you to St Michael's."

Richard Fraser took his guest round to the vicarage and introduced him to his housekeeper Mrs. Hunter and his little Jack Russell dog that jumped and twitched with excitement. "I don't know what is wrong with him today," said the vicar, "he has jumped up and yapped away all morning. It's most unlike him."

Mrs. Wheeler showed Cornelius to his room.

"It was very kind of your husband to come and meet me,'" said Armstrong.

"Oh, that's alright," replied the housekeeper with as much cordiality as her husband had shown an hour earlier. "Anything that keeps him out of mischief," she added with a smile.

Mrs. Hunter then prepared the vicar and the policeman a light lunch before the two prepared to go out on the marsh.

"I've arranged to meet our fellow bird watchers shortly after lunch," said Fraser as they sat down.

At the appointed hour, the two new friends donned their outdoor wear and ventured onto the marsh. They had barely walked a hundred yards when the vicar stopped. "I'm terribly sorry, Cornelius – fool that I am, I've forgotten my field glasses! Could you bear with me while I pop back and get them?"

"Of course," said Armstrong, "I'll wait here." As his gaze followed Richard back to the vicarage, he heard the dog yapping and whining.

Cornelius turned and surveyed the scene in front of him, under what was now a brooding iron-grey sky. The marsh seemed to stretch in every direction, as far as the eye could see, and to merge without a break into the waters of the Solway. Across the Firth there were some fine views of the Scottish hills. Cornelius marveled at the startling beauty of it all; the sense of space and its wide, bare openness with the vastness of the sky above made him feel quite exhilarated.

The wind started to pick up and prompted the calf-length grass to eddy and swirl in mesmerising patterns. There was a sudden rawk-rawk of an unseen bird out on the marsh; Cornelius raised his field glasses to see if he could spot it. As he was scanning the land in front of him, a voice cried out over to his right.

"Hello there, Inspector!"

Armstrong turned his head to see four men standing about fifty yards away. The automatic policeman's scan was almost amused by the eclectic mix: the speaker was a thin man who wore a hairy brown coat and woollen hat, two others stood beside him sporting tweed jackets – one with a flat cap, one without – while a taller man with tousled shoulder length hair stood slightly behind them. All four wore beards – *about the only thing they have in common*, thought Armstrong.

The honking of geese overhead instinctively made Cornelius look up; a skein flew over in a stunning 'V' formation – he watched them until they became a single black speck on the horizon. When he looked back, the thin man was only a few yards away.

"The Reverend said we were to have a visitor from the city. We're all keen bird watchers ourselves, you know," offering a hand. "My name is Michael Turner; I'm the station master here at Burgh. My friends and I have been coming out on to the marsh for more years than we care to remember." He pointed to his colleagues, one of whom was walking away in the direction of the village; another was standing on his own, apparently unsure about something; the taller man was nowhere to be seen.

"Yes, Richard was telling me all about you the other night," said Cornelius, "The King Edward Ghost Hunters? Is that right?"

"Oh yes, it was a name given to us by some of the villagers in the pub who are always teasing us – they always claim we were looking for the late King's ghost. To be honest, I don't believe in ghosts myself, but it keeps the locals amused," said Turner.

"Talking about King Edward, hasn't it led to some study group?" asked the policeman.

"Yes that's right," replied Turner with some enthusiasm, "it was the vicar's suggestion; when we don't fancy bird-watching we do some research into old 'Longshanks'."

"Speak of the devil – the vicar, that is, not 'Longshanks'," said Cornelius, pointing over Turner's shoulder, to the approaching vicar and one of his companions.

"Ah, I see you have met Michael," said Fraser, and then indicated to the man with him, "this is Tom Carmichael, another of our fraternity."

"Cornelius Armstrong,' said the Carlisle man with a handshake.

"How do you do," said Carmichael.

"Are your other friends not joining us," asked the detective with a general nod in the direction of where he first saw them.

The three men from Burgh looked quizzically at one another for a moment.

"The other man was Bill Hartley," said Fraser after a few seconds. "He is a carter and apparently there is a problem with his employer's horse, so he cannot join us."

There was an unusual silence as if the group were talking at cross purposes. Then suddenly a curlew, apparently disturbed by the men, rose from a bracken bush a few yards away and soared aloft into the slate-coloured sky.

"Well gentlemen," said Richard, "that appears to be our signal to start our afternoon's entertainment. Shall we?"

Chapter Five

The Secrets of the Study Group

"Could I propose we call it an afternoon, gentlemen, and retire to my study for something to warm us up?"

The suggestion came after two hours on the marsh and sounded attractive to the vicar's companions; although there was a tacit politeness amongst the recently-acquainted group, there was certainly no appetite among them to refuse such an opportunity to extricate themselves from mother-nature's rawness. The exposed marsh might have provided an interesting few hours bird-watching, but the merciless icy blasts from the Solway made it an unforgiving location – anyone out there for any length of time was rewarded with a bone-chilling coldness that numbed to the very marrow.

It was late afternoon and the already dull day was turning to dusk: the light was fading and the wind began to gust loudly, as if to emphasise the Reverend's belief that it was time to end any outdoor activity. The group made their way back to the vicarage in the gathering gloom.

The study of Reverend Fraser by comparison was warm and welcoming to the birdwatchers, and the blazing fire – kindled by the housekeeper Mrs. Hunter for their arrival – along with the pot of coffee and selection of home-made cakes perked the companions up considerably.

A settee had been positioned with its back to the window; Richard's dog Jack stood on it with his front paws propped up against the back looking out on to the marsh and whinnying constantly.

"Jack, what is wrong with you today?" asked his master. The dog looked from him to the window and back again and shook its hind quarters in nervous excitement.

Inspector Armstrong noticed some papers on the desk entitled *Study Group Notes*. "Oh, I remember you telling me about your study group, Richard," he said pointing to them.

"Yes, we are having some great fun," enthused Fraser, "Tom here and Bill Hartley are even talking about going to Scotland later in the year as part of our studies."

"I'm sure that will be very nice," said Armstrong, turning to Tom Carmichael who smiled and nodded but didn't elaborate. "So how long have you been studying the life of Edward?" asked Cornelius.

"For about two months now, I suppose," replied Reverend Fraser, who received a confirming nod from his friends and parishioners. "We have quite a little group going: Tom and Michael here, Bill, who had to leave earlier, Sam Hunter, who picked you up at Kirkandrews, and one or two others who have a passing interest."

"And what have you found out?"

"We have had tremendous success already, Inspector, due in no small part to the help of the chap in the Library archives at...oh, what is it called again?" he asked turning to his companions.

'Tullie House,' replied Turner.

"Oh, you mean Sydney Irvine?" said Cornelius, "I know Sydney well – he has helped me with many a query."

"Yes, that's the fellow," said Richard, "a lovely chap. He even allowed us to borrow some of the documents for our group."

The vicar then took great delight in apprising the policeman of the group's own detective work so far: "It seems that Edward visited Carlisle many times during the last twenty years of his life following the death of the Scottish King Alexander III," and then picking up a book on the period, began to read, "'...when Alexander's young granddaughter and sole heir died, Edward chose John Balliol as the new King of Scotland in 1291. Balliol's subjects were none too happy with the arrangement and rebelled against the king and his master south of the border. Balliol then embarked on a futile attempt to placate both his countrymen and his king but only succeeded in exposing himself as weak and indecisive. After five years, King Edward's patience ran out and he marched north to deal with the rebellious Scots himself; he had Balliol sent to London and locked him in the Tower for good measure. Balliol's humiliation was complete when Edward had the Stone of Destiny – a venerated relic, which Scottish Kings had been crowned on since the Dark Ages – removed from Scone to Westminster Abbey, where it still lies.' Wonderful stuff!" said Fraser as he moved across to a strong box that sat in the corner of his study. "This is my particular favourite however," he said producing a delicate brown parchment. He laid it out on the table in front of his guests. "We have had tremendous fun trying to decipher the content."

The calligraphic writing was difficult to make sense of and the faded ink on the decaying paper turned the task into a genuine decoding operation.

"We believe it is a reference to Robert the Bruce's visit to Carlisle to meet with King Edward in 1297. See here," he continued, pointing out the numbers '2' and '9' that could clearly be seen, "and here, the name 'Brus'. It is difficult to date the document; the best we can offer is that it was written during one of the Parliament sessions that were held in the castle in early 1307, shortly before the King's death."

"And who do you think it would be written by?" asked Armstrong.

"Our investigations are continuing, Inspector," laughed the vicar.

"*Hmm'*" mused Cornelius, leaning on the table and resting his chin on his upturned hand, "Am I right in saying that Bruce was allied to Edward at one point?"

"He certainly was my dear Cornelius," replied Richard, "Bruce and his father initially sided with Edward against Balliol whom they considered a slippery usurper. That is why he came to Carlisle in 1297 to swear his allegiance to the English Crown."

"Little did he know that he would be meeting his future nemesis," mumbled Cornelius, half to himself.

"Indeed," concluded Richard, "their alliance didn't last long it would seem. Ten years later Bruce would have the last laugh on Edward: old Longshanks was on his way to fight the Scots, after Bruce was declared King, when he breathed his last out on the marsh."

"So how do you see your studies progressing?" asked Armstrong, slightly altering his line of questioning.

"Oh, there is always something of interest," said Michael Turner, "take Tom here – he and Bill Hartley are looking into a character who was found hanging from the bell tower in the Cathedral not long after the King's death."

"Really, how did you find out about him," asked the policeman.

"Well we were looking through some documents at Tullie House when I saw a reference to some bloke called William Hartley who it was thought had been murdered by Simon somebody-or-other."

"Yes," added Fraser with a smile, "according to George Hammond, the Head Verger at the Cathedral, his ghost can still be seen wandering round the bell tower."

"Well, because our own Bill Hartley shares the same name," resumed Turner "he and Tom have been trying to find out what went on."

"And what have you found?" asked Armstrong, turning to Carmichael.

"Awe, not much really," he replied.

The group continued chatting about the period in history for some time before Turner and Carmichael took their leave.

Armstrong and Fraser enjoyed a hearty meal as the wind gusted across the desolate plain outside.

"How about a game of chess and a night-cap?" suggested the Reverend.

"Oh, I don't know about that, Richard, I haven't played chess in years," replied Cornelius.

"You must," insisted his host with a smile, "I rarely have visitors and I do so love a game of chess. Do indulge me, Inspector."

Unable to resist the charm of his new friend, Armstrong acquiesced, and soon began to regret his decision: the Reverend quickly became the picture of concentration, engaging in strict self-analysis and reproach. Not that there was much need for reproach – he proceeded to dismantle his opponent with successive calm, steady moves. Cornelius's moves by comparison seemed random and nonsensical, achieving, if anything, no more than short-term gain.

"I used to think I was reasonably good at this," he said after a while, "When I learned how to play, I thought the aim was to entertain oneself, not to humiliate one's opponent!"

"I'm sorry, Cornelius, I do have a rather shameful competitive streak in me," replied an embarrassed Fraser, with his characteristic grin. "I mean no harm, I assure you."

"I bet you say that to all the Grand Masters you beat," quipped Cornelius, to their amusement.

"I thought that chap Tom Carmichael was rather quiet," commented the policeman, reverting to the events of earlier in the afternoon.

"Yes, I noticed that," replied Richard, "he's normally a talkative character. He must have been missing his good pal, Bill."

"Yes, what happened to him and the other chap I saw earlier this afternoon? They didn't hang around long."

"I'm not sure," said the Reverend, a little confused, "you met the group when I popped back into the house. When I returned I saw Bill walking away – Tom said he had 'something on'. I never saw anyone else."

125

The two ended the evening with a hand shake and once again wishing each other a 'Happy New Year.' Cornelius retired to his comfortable room, prepared for him by Mrs. Hunter. As he was putting on his nightshirt, a gust of wind rattled the window and the guttering candle that stood on the table before it flickered uneasily until, on the verge of being extinguished, it flared vigorously into life again. Cornelius went over to check the latch on the window; as he did so, he heard a high pitched squeaking outside. Like all detectives, Armstrong was not renowned for his lack of curiosity; he moved the candle to the bedside table, lifted the window open and leant out into the inky blackness to see where the noises were coming from. Something swooped past causing him to involuntarily duck; then another! Just before him, they veered to the left, rising and swirling, and then they spiraled downwards sinking into the ground. Not birds, he realised, but bats.

Cornelius pulled the window back down, fastened the clasp, drew the curtains and blew out the candle. "That's just enough for one day," he said to himself and climbed into bed.

Chapter Six

Carlisle Cathedral, 1297

The Reverend Richard Fraser and his friends were wrong about the mysterious parchment they had discovered in the archives. It was not written – as they had suspected – during one of the Parliament sessions of 1307; it had been written on another freezing January night, some ten years earlier in 1297. The chronicler was Rodger de Coventry, the Treasurer of King Edward I.

It was written during Coventry's third visit to Carlisle as part of Edward's court.

Rodger was the grandson of a French nobleman; his mother had married a courtier of Edward's father Henry III. He was two years older than the King, and had served his master for approaching thirty years, having been part of the young Prince Edward's entourage, when he went on his crusade to the Holy Land in 1270. He then came to the prince's attention in May of the following year when Edward was attacked by a would-be assassin at Acre; it was Coventry and a few other courtiers who were on hand to wrestle the assailant to ground. Coventry grew ever closer over the following years, and when Edward was crowned King in 1274, Rodger was rewarded with the illustrious position of King's Treasurer. He established a reputation as a skilled administrator when – during the first fifteen years of the King's reign – he oversaw the building of a granite ring of castles around the western and northern coasts of Wales, from where Edward's troops could control the rebellious locals; and effectively implemented the King's taxation reforms in order to generate financial support for Edward's numerous military campaigns.

Four months earlier, Coventry had been with Edward in Berwick to accept Robert the Bruce's declaration of loyalty to the English crown; now he was in Carlisle on a cold afternoon in January 1297 to see the Scot confirm his allegiance.

The interior of the cathedral was spartan; wall-mounted torches burned along the inner walls and the main aisle but provided little light and even less warmth for the numerous vassals and burgesses who had gathered in the cavernous church to witness the historic event. Scores of men lined each side of the main aisle, creating a natural passageway from the main door to the altar. Behind them, with their backs against the outer walls were numerous spearmen and archers. A weak, wintery sun filtered through the East Window and over the altar on to the back of a lone individual – a tall, bearded, dark haired figure, with a swarthy complexion and fiery Plantagenet eyes, and dressed in a long deep-red cloak: King Edward.

Within three paces to the left of Edward stood a valet holding the King's Standard – its splashes of red, blue and gold in contrast to the otherwise sepulchral shades of the building and multitude gathered within it. Of equal distance to the King's right stood his personal body guard, armed with a loaded cross bow. It was mid-afternoon by the time his visitor arrived.

Robert the Bruce was himself an impressive figure; politically intelligent and militarily successful, he commanded a presence in keeping with his upbringing and heritage. Both he and his father had refused to back John Balliol as King of Scotland and supported Edward's invasion of Scotland the previous year. The two titans of the age had met five months earlier at the 'victory parliament' in Berwick; now Bruce was in Carlisle to reiterate his loyalty to Edward. He entered the cathedral with his retinue and walked slowly and silently through the gauntlet of Knights towards the solitary figure at its head. Stopping within an arm's length, he knelt and addressed his monarch in his heavy Scots brogue.

"My Lord," he said, "I have come to declare fealty to you and your crown."

For his part, the King recognised the support he had received from the Bruce Family in the past – he had even appointed Robert's father as Constable of Carlisle Castle two years earlier. But he viewed the man who knelt before him with some suspicion, as he was aware that Bruce was supporting the other Scottish talisman, William Wallace, who was intent on stoking the embers of revolt against the English.

"What have you for me?" said the King without ceremony.

Bruce gestured to one of his entourage who stepped forward with a strongbox; as he did so the King's bodyguard instinctively adjusted his grip on the cross-bow.

"Here, My Lord, are the monies owed to you by my father," said Bruce, "and details of the treasures hidden by the traitor Balliol."

"Of what treasures do you speak?" asked Edward.

"Sire," replied the Bruce, "Balliol spent most of his reign making sure his own dealings were well stocked. When he married some years ago, he got his greedy hands on a massive dowry, including much silver and gold, put up by his wife's father, the Earl of Surrey. I believe he still has the Seal of the Kingdom of Scotland and much of his silver and gold is hidden away; or it was until I found out about it. The details of where are contained here."

He offered the box to the King.

"Coventry?" called the King

A broad man with a big red beard appeared through the crowed of nobility.

"Sire."

"Take this box and ensure its safekeeping," then, turning back to Bruce, "I acknowledge your fealty, Lord Bruce. You are welcome in my kingdom."

With that, the ceremony was over.

That night, safely ensconced in the Royal Quarters, Rodger de Coventry made an inventory of the box's contents. Inside were six leather bags of silver coins, and many documents detailing the various locations throughout Galloway where John Balliol had apparently hidden away his various riches. The King's Treasurer then proceeded to consolidate all of these entries into one document; he then bundled them together, placing his own summary on top and tied the papers together with a thin band of leather. The box was then locked and marked with the King's seal.

Once Coventry had performed his official duties, he set about fulfilling his own. An avid diarist, he had already chronicled in some detail his master's visits to Palestine and Egypt; to France and Sicily. Now he recorded the historic visit to Carlisle of Robert the Bruce to pay homage to his King.

The following day, Coventry called his assistant Simon Ashbourne to his rooms and handed him the small chest with its valuable contents. Ashbourne was a distinctive figure around the court as he was the only member who stood in excess of six feet tall – as tall as the King himself.

"In keeping with custom," Coventry said to his aide, "the contents of this box should remain in this shire in the King's name and should only be used to uphold his rule in this area. Take it to the Burgess of the Cathedral to be added to the monies locked in the crypt."

"What did you find in there, My Lord," asked the inquisitive assistant.

Coventry enjoyed the King's trust; he had gained it by demonstrating his honesty and discretion for many years, and he had no intention of compromising that trust by divulging his master's accounts – even to one of his own aids. He gave a long look at Simon. "A plentiful amount," he said, "all of which concerns neither you nor me. You have your instructions, Ashbourne."

"Yes, My Lord," replied Simon, who had himself witnessed the previous day's events, and, more significantly heard the exchange between the Edward and Robert, and the latter's reference to Balliol's treasure.

He sought out William Hartley whom he knew due to his visiting Carlisle several times as part of the King's Court.

Hartley was a local dignitary who resented the fact that he had twice been overlooked for positions he felt were appropriate for a man of his standing: first was the King's decision to look elsewhere for a Sheriff of Cumberland six years earlier, and then four years later when Edward appointed Robert the Bruce's father as Constable of Carlisle Castle. Hartley instead had to satisfy himself with the comparatively lowly position of Burgess of the Cathedral.

Hartley took Ashbourne down an open stone staircase in the cathedral to the crypt. Selecting one of the keys on a large ring, he opened the thick, arch-shaped timber door and escorted his visitor inside. Whatever light filtered down from the church above was virtually extinguished, forcing Hartley to light a candle as he was used to doing in such circumstances. He then locked the door behind them. At the far end of the crypt was a similar door to the one they had just passed through; Hartley led Ashbourne across the stone floor and repeated the practice. The chamber in which the two now found themselves was the Cathedral Treasury.

Bags of coins and Diocesan silver were piled on top of one another throughout the room. Ashbourne's avaricious eyes surveyed the contents, as he placed the King's chest on the floor.

"It appears the church is in good wealth?" he said.

"Yes," agreed Hartley balefully, "and it's left to people like me to guard it for them. Not that I am likely to see any reward."

"It is people like you and me who deserve a little more reward, if you ask me," said Ashbourne, surveying the contents of the cellar.

The Burgess held up his candle, so its soft light illuminated the face of his companion who smiled thinly; Hartley studied his companion carefully. "That is dangerous talk, Master Ashbourne."

"Just thinking aloud, Master Hartley," replied Ashbourne with a shrug, "just thinking aloud."

Simon Ashbourne was destined to make a mental note of the various pots of treasure King Edward secreted away around the country over the next ten years. His words to the Burgess of Carlisle Cathedral in that dark cellar in January 1297 meanwhile, and the sense of injustice experienced by the latter over the years were destined to gnaw away at William Hartley for the next decade.

Chapter Seven

Innocent Private Investigations

Cornelius Armstrong yawned, stretched and stared out of the window he had hung out of the night before; there were no signs of bats or any other wildlife on this frosty morning. An immaculate spider's web that had been spun on the exterior of the window, at the corner of the mullion and the lintel, had turned into what looked like beads of thick cotton wool.

"I saw bats last night before I went to bed," said Cornelius as he met his host for breakfast.

"Yes, we have a resident colony," replied Richard with a smile, "they apparently roost in the bell tower. All adds to the gothic mystery of the place, I suppose."

The two enjoyed a hearty breakfast before Cornelius took his leave. As the trains were running again after the holiday, Armstrong made his way to the platform of the small village station and inevitably met the Station Master, Michael Turner, whose company he had enjoyed the previous afternoon. The two chatted for a while before the train that ran along the old canal line between Port Carlisle and the city arrived shortly after ten o'clock. Cornelius made the short train journey home and prepared to resume his normal duties after the holiday break.

Those duties proved to be relatively mundane as the New Year progressed, and as winter turned to spring. A series of burglaries at the Pawn Shop on Water Street in Wapping proved a relatively straightforward case once Inspector Armstrong had gleaned some vital information from his informant Reuben Hanks; while a claim of slander against a reputable shopkeeper, in the local press, ultimately proved to be one of simple mistaken identity – the man had the singular misfortune of sharing his name with that of an escaped prisoner from Durham Gaol.

Then an unusual happenstance occurred on the first Saturday morning in May, when Cornelius was enjoying a day off. As he often did, he visited the City Library across Abbey Street at Tullie House, to browse the shelves for something different, or to look through the reference section. As he ambled around one of the tall stands he came face to face with two men, one of whom stopped in his tracks at the sight of the policeman.

"Hello," ventured Armstrong, searching for the man's name.

"Hello," replied the man, furtively.

"Tom...isn't it? ...Carmichael. From Burgh?"

"Yes, that's right, Inspector Armstrong," said Carmichael, who obviously had no difficulty remembering the man who visited Burgh Marsh on New Year's Day. Apparently feeling obliged to introduce his companion, he added, "this is Bill Hartley, who couldn't join us on the day."

"Yes I remember now, there was yourself and the other man who had something else on," said Cornelius, with an outstretched hand and trying to remember the sequence of events.

Unlike his wiry companion, Hartley was of stocky build; he appeared to be a surly individual with intense, beady eyes. "How do?" he said.

"What brings you to town?" asked Armstrong, and then with instant realisation answered his own question, "oh, you will be looking into your study group?"

"Yes that's right," said Carmichael, without elaborating.

"And what have you found out lately?" Armstrong noticed he had a battered dullish-green book under his arm.

"Oh, not much really."

The three men stood for several seconds nodding and smiling in an uncomfortable silence, before Armstrong put them out of their misery.

"Well I'll let you get away."

"Yes, we must be going," said Carmichael, "nice to see you again."

Hartley gave a simple nod and Armstrong watched the two men walk away, puzzled by the exchange. It did succeed however, in making up the mind of the inquisitive detective regarding what he wanted to look at that morning: the life of Edward I and his time in the Carlisle area. He sought out the librarian.

Sydney Irvine was an elderly gentleman, probably in his early sixties. He had a thin snowy thatch of hair that was raked over to cover his balding crown, and possessed an alert but homely face, with high arched eyebrows; he wore a cardigan that looked as old as he was. Sydney had worked in the library for as long as Cornelius could remember – one of life's fixed points in a seemingly ever changing world. He smiled at the policeman's request to see any papers that were available in the archives.

"They are proving extremely popular, I must say. There were two gentlemen earlier who seem to spend more and more time here pouring over whatever documents they can get their hands on. I think they are part of some group out at Burgh."

"Yes, I've met them," said Cornelius. "What sort of things have they been looking at?"

"Come with me, Inspector."

He led Cornelius down a metal staircase into the basement of the library; they walked the length of the building between the ceiling-high shelves, stacked with books and ledgers. Armstrong, the avid amateur historian was in his element, intrigued and excited by what he was about to learn. At the end of the corridor of shelving, there was a study area, with three tables and four large map drawer chests. Adjacent to this area was a locked door; Sydney took out a bunch of keys from his cardigan pocket and studied them carefully.

"When I've met other members of the group, they ask to see more general information about Edward and his court when they were in Carlisle in the late thirteenth and early fourteenth centuries." He selected one of the keys and opened the door and indicated that Cornelius should follow him inside. "Those two gentlemen seem obsessed by the King's death however," he said reaching up to one of the high shelves. "They have prompted me over the past few months to sort through the various papers and correspondence of the day."

An ancient mustiness padded the air, and as the Librarian disturbed the shelves and pulled down some of the papers, dust threatened to cover the two men. "These are some of the papers I have recently catalogued," he said as the two emerged from the cloud and back into the study area. He untied the bundles and laid out the papers on one of the tables and invited the off-duty detective to sit down. "There you go, Mr. Armstrong," he said turning to resume his other duties, "that should keep you quiet for an hour or two."

Cornelius scanned the documents: parchments, similar to the one he had seen in Reverend Fraser's study some months earlier; cognisance from Edward's Parliament that was held in Carlisle during the period; and even the work of chroniclers of the day. Taking his magnifying lens, Armstrong decided to try and pick out significant events in chronological order.

He read a piece signed by a man called Rodger de Coventry who was apparently the King's Treasurer. Coventry gave a detailed eye-witness account of Robert the Bruce's visit to Carlisle to declare fealty to the King in 1297. *I wonder if this document was written at the same time as the one Richard showed me*, Cornelius thought as he picked his way through Coventry's beautiful calligraphy. But – like the two members of the study group he had encountered earlier – he found himself quickly moving forward to 1307: the year of the King's death.

Historians over the centuries narrated how relations had deteriorated between Edward and Bruce in the final ten years of the King's life, and it was Edward's final Scottish campaign that had brought him back to the Border City.

Parliament had been summoned to meet in the city on the 20th January 1307, but the King, who had been ill for some time, was unable to leave Lanercost Priory to make the final ten-mile journey to Carlisle; Parliament was therefore adjourned. It was the second week in March by the time Edward was healthy enough to attend.

Cornelius sifted through several covenants, deeds and charters, mainly dealing with financial matters, and noted that there was plenty of representation from Barons who were unhappy with the King's apparently regular demands for increases in taxes. He noted that most of this documentation was dealt with by a courtier called Simon Ashbourne.

The detective reached into his waistcoat pocket, pulled out his watch and flicked open the cover. He was surprised to see that it was three o'clock – he had been down there for four hours; his stomach rumbled, as if to remind him that he had missed his lunch. He gave his face a dry rub with both hands and had decided it was time to call it a day when his eye fell upon an account of King Edward's death by a contemporary diarist, apparently written some ten years later. Cornelius couldn't resist reading the piece – he felt it was this sort of document that made history live and breathe.

The record spoke of the 'Indomitable King' who left Carlisle on horseback on 26th June. The warrior King must have been in agony as he was transferred to a litter that took six days to reach Kirkandrews-on-Eden. Struggling on to Burgh by Sands, '...the King breathed his last on 7th July.' Edward's body lay in state in St Michael's Church at Burgh before the long trek back to London for burial at Westminster Abbey. The Prince of Wales hurried down from Scotland when he heard of his father's death, paying homage to the body at Burgh before being proclaimed King Edward II the following day at Carlisle.

Cornelius read of the unusual post script to the narrative: two days after the King's death, his courtier Simon Ashbourne was suspected of murdering The Burgess of

Carlisle Cathedral – a William Hartley – by hanging him from the bell tower. Armstrong remembered the study group mentioning something about Hartley and the coincidence of one of the group sharing his name.

The piece stated that Ashbourne was a particularly tall man, '...the only man in court to rival the height of the King himself.' It concluded by stating that Ashbourne stole some treasures from the crypt of the Cathedral and was never seen or heard of again.

Cornelius Armstrong sat in the dimly lit basement of Tullie House Library, staring into the middle distance and twisting the horns of his moustache: a sure sign that he had much to ponder.

Chapter Eight

Sinister Private Investigations

"Of all the people we had to bump into, we had to bump into him."

Tom Carmichael was thinking aloud but he could have been speaking for both himself and his friend as they walked out of Tullie House on that lovely May morning.

"I know," agreed Bill Hartley, "the less he knows the better. I thought after his visit to the vicarage that would be the last we saw of him."

"Never mind," said Carmichael, as the two walked through the Abbey Gate into the Cathedral grounds on their way to the station. "He can't possibly suspect anything – what is there to suspect?"

"Mmm." Hartley looked at his colleague with less assurance.

As they walked past the main door of the Cathedral on their left and the site of the old Chapter House on their right, both men slowed to a halt and looked across at the large detached house that stood on its own within the grounds, and masked St Cuthbert's Church beyond.

"That's the Head Verger's House," Carmichael said pointing. "What do you think?"

"I have a good feeling about this, Tom," replied his companion. He continued, pointing, "I reckon if there *is* anything to find, it could be under that house." He turned towards what would have been the old Nave. "See?" he said sweeping his arm back and forward creating an imaginary diagonal line across the ground between the cathedral and the house within The Abbey.

Carmichael took the book from under his arm and opened it at a page he had marked by turning down the top right hand corner. He studied a drawing on the page for some time and then compared it with the signal Hartley was making.

"I think you're right, Bill," he said after a while, "but how are we going to find out?"

"Where there's a will, there's a way," said his friend. "We'll just have to go home and have a think about it."

That afternoon, back in the village, the two men met up with their study group colleagues in *The Lowther Arms*. What had started the previous year upon a suggestion from the new vicar as a mildly interesting past time, had developed into a serious hobby that saw the group debating sincerely about the king and his court, and the influence it had had on Carlisle and the surrounding area. Moreover, what were the legacies and influences that had been left in the area by such an auspicious presence?

Each of the group had their own favourite topic: not surprisingly, Reverend Fraser found himself gravitating towards the theological influences of the day, while Michael Turner, the Station Master, had a particular interest in the parliaments that were held in Carlisle. Sam Hunter, blacksmith and husband of Fraser's housekeeper, meanwhile, was drawn in by the general Anglo-Scottish relations and the battles they inevitably led to. Unknown to their friends however, Carmichael and Hartley were carrying out their own investigations: a legacy of a different kind had grabbed their interest.

To their colleagues, they were becoming more and more reticent about their interest, preferring simply to participate in general conversation about the subjects their friends would raise on any given afternoon. What their fellow villagers perceived as a general diminishing of interest in the subject matter, was actually a deliberate attempt to mislead them and clear the way for the two to benefit from information they were withholding.

Some weeks before Christmas, Michael Turner had discovered information about Bill Hartley's namesake who had been murdered by a member of the King's Court.

"You wanna be careful, Bill," said Turner with laugh, "you don't wanna end up like that last bloke called Hartley who got involved."

There was much merriment and leg-pulling amongst the friends. Had Turner read on however, he would have learned that the courtier concerned had made off with some of the king's treasure via a disused drainage system deep under the cathedral and its grounds; neither the courtier concerned nor the treasure had ever been seen again.

Significantly, Hartley had read the piece after Turner had passed it to him and he showed it to Carmichael. This led to Carmichael referring to a battered old history of Carlisle Cathedral that he possessed. In the book there was a reference to the drainage system; there were several instances of the underground tunnels collapsing before they were finally decommissioned at the time of the great fire in 1292. Three cellars were constructed under appropriate buildings within The Abbey some ten years later, to gain access to the unstable shafts, in order to effect repair but there was no further record of them ever being used.

As the weeks passed, the two gradually centered their studies on the courtier in question: Simon Ashbourne. What interested the pair was the fact that Ashbourne had murdered Hartley and apparently fled with the small chest containing what they believed to be references to where John Balliol had hidden various treasures when he was being hounded by King Edward.

The more they read up on the subject, the more convinced they became of a particular hypothesis: what if Ashbourne did not escape? What if he had become trapped in the collapsed tunnels deep under the grounds of the Cathedral?

At first Hartley thought it was too fanciful, but Carmichael gradually made a strong case to his friend.

"Think about it, Bill. No one saw or heard of Ashbourne again; no one ever recovered Balliol's treasure, despite it being common knowledge that he had stockpiles all throughout Galloway; we know the drainage system that was put in after the fire of 1292 was poorly constructed and there are many references to the tunnels collapsing before it was finally condemned in the early 1300s. I wonder if maybe – just maybe – Ashbourne murders Hartley and then tries to make his escape through the drainage tunnel, only for it to collapse and trap him?"

"It seems a bit far-fetched doesn't it?" asked his sceptical friend.

The two continued the debate for some weeks before they came across a particular parchment among many within the archives that referred to William Hartley's groom being placed in the stocks: '...while his master was found done to death by hanging two days following the death of the king, this man did leave two of his master's horses unattended outside the city walls.'

"What do you make of that then?" cried Carmichael when he read account. "That has to be too much of a coincidence – Hartley has his man place horses outside the walls for the escape."

"But Hartley was murdered?" questioned his nineteenth century namesake.

"Well maybe he was in on it after all," countered Carmichael. "Come to think of it, how would Ashbourne get into the treasury and know about the drainage system without the help of the local man. I reckon once Hartley had served his purpose, Ashbourne bumps him off and tries to make his escape. I'm telling you Bill, that bugger's still down there, and more importantly, so are those treasure maps."

"It does all fit together, I'll grant you that," said Hartley thoughtfully. "What are you proposing?"

"I wonder if we can get underground somehow to see if there is anything there."

"Well, that book says that there are deep cellars under a few of them houses," said Hartley, warming to the idea. "If we could access one, we might be able to get down there."

During one of their many trips to Carlisle, they visited the cathedral and encountered an official with a high forehead and a haughty demeanour who was poring over a book and some papers on a desk inside the main door.

"Excuse me," said Hartley, "could you tell me anything about the drainage system in the cathedral, please?"

The man raised his head and peered disdainfully over the top of a pair of half-moon glasses that hung precariously from his long nose. He looked Hartley up and down and then repeated the practice with Carmichael. After an interminable pause he spoke.

"The drainage system? Why do you want to know about the drainage system?" His tone had a disdain he made no attempt to disguise.

"Awe, we're just a couple of builders from out Moorehouse way and we're putting some drains in. It just got us thinking about how those old boys built services for structures like this."

The man seemed less than convinced about the story but decided the best way to get rid of these nuisances was to answer their question and send them on their way. "The drainage system has been overhauled several times over the centuries; the most recent system was installed fifty years ago."

"Did I hear that there were some collapsed drains at one time?" persisted Hartley.

"Yes," replied the man curtly, clearly growing tired by the conversation, "at the time of the great fire."

"And the cellars that were used to service these drains – are they still in operation?"

"No they are not," said the man sharply, "they haven't been accessed for centuries. Now if you will excuse me I am extremely busy."

With that, he snapped the book shut that lay in front of him on the desk, stood up and walked off in the direction of the chancel.

The more the days and weeks went by, the more the two read around the subject, and the more they became convinced that their hypothesis was sound. Moreover, they began to believe it could lead to them discovering riches in Scotland that no one was even aware of. By the time Carmichael and Hartley encountered Inspector Armstrong in Tullie House on that May morning, they were actively looking for a way to get into the subterranean passages under the Cathedral.

Chapter Nine

Searching Underground

Like Carmichael and Hartley, Cornelius Armstrong was becoming increasingly intrigued with what lay below medieval Carlisle. Still unaware that the members of the study group had anything other than a curious interest in Longshanks's period, Armstrong had become drawn further into his own studies after stimulating his inquisitiveness in the library.

He was puzzled by the riddle involving Simon Ashbourne and it crossed his mind that there might still be some clues in the passages and drainage systems he had read about; so much so that he decided to broach the subject with his friend and superior Chief Constable Henry Baker. Knocking and putting his head round the door of Baker's office he asked, "Sir, can I have a quick word?"

"Certainly," replied Baker beckoning him inside. When Armstrong deliberately closed the door behind him, the Chief Constable added, "this looks serious. Everything alright, Cornelius?"

Once inside and out of ear-shot of colleagues, Armstrong dropped the formalities. "Yes, fine, it's just a non-work matter," he said a little embarrassed; then after a slight pause he continued,

"Henry, can I ask you a silly question?"

"That's not really the sort of thing I want to hear from my best detective," said the Chief Constable with a smile.

Armstrong ignored the teasing, "'Remember at your Christmas party you told the story about the Blackfriars and the ghost – is there any truth in that?"

Baker burst out laughing causing Armstrong to look over his shoulder to make sure the door was firmly closed. "You never cease to surprise me, Cornelius! For such an excellent detective, you possess a naïveté that is irresistible. It's a wonder the ladies don't fall over themselves to get at you!"

"That's a 'no' then?" said Armstrong feeling suitably foolish.

"Of course, it was absolute nonsense – just a little bit of after dinner fun on the evening and an opportunity to see a few of the ladies jump out of their skin at the desired moments. Why do you ask, for goodness sake?"

"Oh, it's just a little bit of research I've been doing recently dating back to Edward I's time and various references to some underground passageways round this area."

"Ah!!!" cried Baker.

"What is it?"

"I've just realised now why the ladies don't fall over themselves to get at you!"

"Very funny, I'm sure," said Cornelius with a forced smile and nod.

"Seriously then," continued Baker, "the bit about the Blackfriar's ghost was nonsense but the bit about the hidden passages and cellars is perfectly true. In fact later in the evening Slater the Theatre Manager told me that you can still gain access to one of them deep in the bowels of the theatre. You want to go and ask him, I'm sure he'll let you have a look."

"That's really interesting, I think I will," said Armstrong thoughtfully.

"What is so interesting?" asked Baker.

"I'm not sure, really. I just find myself being drawn into some unsolved mystery – I don't know where it's going to lead."

"Can I remind you Inspector that we have plenty of modern day mysteries to solve, without travelling back in time to find out who did what with their red-hot pokers!"

"I understand, Henry," said Cornelius with his hand on the door knob, "I will carry out my investigations in my own time." He left his superior shaking his head and laughing to himself.

*****

Some days later, at an appropriate time, Cornelius did call on Robert Slater as his friend had suggested. Explaining his interest, Slater couldn't resist a cynical swipe, "Still looking for ghosts from the past eh?"' he said with a crooked smile.

Armstrong made no attempt to justify his interest and quickly changed the subject by asking how Mrs. Slater was, as he was taken down a tatty old staircase into the basement of the theatre.

"Fine," said Slater. He opened a wooden hatch in the floor of the basement that revealed another flight of steps which dropped away into the darkness. "If you go down there," he said, "you will see a large hole in the West Wall. I think it is where the drains used to empty out into the dam. Anyway, I believe it leads to a couple of passageways. Never been down there myself – a bit hooney if you ask me."

"I thought you didn't believe in the super-natural?" asked Armstrong. It was his turn to be mischievous.

It wasn't lost on Slater, "Touché," he said with some magnanimity. "'I'll leave you to it."

Armstrong lit his paraffin lamp and began to descend the few narrow stone stairs that led into a black void. Slater watched from above as the meager glow of the lamp faded into nothingness.

"Are you alright down there, Inspector?" he asked as the light disappeared completely.

"Yes, fine," echoed Armstrong's voice back up through the slim opening, "it is just as you described. I think I will explore a little further if you don't mind."

"Not at all," said Slater, "I'll leave you to it. I'll leave this hatch open – just come out when you are ready. If you are not back in half an hour I'll come back and check you are alright."

"Thanks again," came the voice.

Deep under the theatre Cornelius had located the large hole Slater had told him about. He stood on a stone square at the base of the dozen or so steps; the round entrance to the hole was waist high as he stood on the stone and about four feet in diameter. He raised his lamp to head height and peered through into what he believed was a passageway beyond.

Nothing.

"Well, I've come this far..." he mumbled to himself.

He leant in and placed the lamp on the floor of the tunnel as far as he could reach; then, placing the palms of both hands on the lip of the entrance, he levered himself up off the ground and clambered inside. Picking up his lamp again he edged forward into the inky blackness. Despite the pleasant June temperature at ground level, Cornelius instantly realised how desperately cold it was in this underground corridor; he shivered but at the same time commended himself for having the foresight to put on his woollen cap and outdoor walking coat.

He pressed on with his raised lantern, slightly hunched, one step at a time. After about twenty paces he stopped and looked behind him – any shaft of light from the theatre cellar had disappeared. After a few more paces, he discovered an apparent junction in the passageway where two tunnels seemed to form a Y shape; the tunnel to the left had been blocked up. Priding himself on a decent sense of direction, Cornelius deduced that this must have been the old drain that ran diagonally from the Cathedral out into the old dam beneath the West Walls. *It is true then, I wonder where the other one goes?*

After a few more paces along the right hand tunnel, he found a slight step down into a chamber that he estimated was six or seven paces square. The air was stale and damp, and his breath condensed into thin clouds visible against the glow of the lamp. He estimated he must be somewhere under Blackfriars Street and therefore under the old convent.

He thought back to Baker's story about the monks hiding from their persecutors: *This must have been where they hid*. The damp brick walls glistened and even in the dim light, Cornelius could pick out the slimy traces of snails that had made the dungeon their home over the centuries; the floor was slippery.

Armstrong's mind started to wander to why he was down here in the first place: *if Ashbourne had escaped it is conceivable that he could have made his escape from the walled city through the condemned tunnel*. After a while he smiled to himself, realising that here he was, standing in the dark, a hundred feet or more underground, trying to solve a mystery that dated back some six centuries.

He realised also that he was starting to tremble with the cold. The silence was oppressive and when Cornelius thought he heard a faint scratching sound, he felt it was time to leave this place. He retraced his steps and breathed a great sigh of relief when he managed to lever himself out of the tunnel and back onto the stone platform. As he was climbing the steps back into the basement of the theatre, he was met by Slater who was coming to check on the progress of his guest.

"Any luck?" he asked as the policeman emerged.

"Yes, very interesting," said Cornelius, "but you're right – a bit hooney! No good if you are scared of the dark or suffer from claustrophobia."

"I am curious," said Slater, "but I'm not *that* curious."

Inspector Armstrong thanked Slater for his help and made his way home to Abbey Street. Despite the pleasant June night he asked if Mrs. Wheeler would make up a fire for him. He didn't elaborate on why he was so cold but his housekeeper assumed he'd been "...up to no good, judging by the state of your trousers and your coat. Honestly," she continued as she picked up the offending garments to be taken away and cleaned, "you men are like la'al lads – you never grow up!"

"Thank you Mrs. Wheeler," said Cornelius, suitably contrite, as she closed the door behind her. He lit his long-stemmed pipe and sunk into his rocking chair by the fire.

Chapter Ten

Faces in the Crowd

A month after Armstrong thought he had exhausted all avenues of investigation regarding the cathedral and its hidden past, he found himself being pulled back towards it once more. In the weeks prior to July 1907, he spent as much time as he could with his cousin George, knowing that it would not be long before the Border Regiment soldier would be leaving for a posting overseas. The 2nd Battalion had returned to the Carlisle Depot earlier in the year and now it was time for Sergeant Armstrong's 1st Battalion to leave on a tour that would see them serve abroad in Gibraltar, India and Burma over the next several years.

Finally, on 1st July, it was time for departure. As always at times like these, the city came out to wish their Regiment well; thousands lined the streets as the classic military parade left from the Castle at ten o'clock precisely and marched the short distance to the Cathedral for a thanksgiving service, before marching on toward the station and departure.

Cornelius had said his farewells to George the previous night but still positioned himself opposite the entrance to the Cathedral to give his cousin a final send off. He stood among a throng of cheering and tearful friends and relatives who had come to do the same for their loved ones.

The wave of noise that travelled down Castle Street indicated to those in the grounds that the soldiers' arrival was imminent. As Cornelius stood waiting amidst the noisy and waving multitude that flanked each side of the driveway from the street to the main door, his eye bizarrely picked out the two men he had seen in the library two months earlier among the scores of people who stood with their backs to the Cathedral on the opposite side of the driveway. It took some moments for their vaguely familiar faces to register with him and he was amazed that he should pick them out among such a large crowd.

I wonder what they are doing here? There was no sign of any other relatives with them so it was unlikely that they had someone in the Regiment who was leaving. What's more, when Armstrong looked closer, he sensed that they were not behaving like the hundreds of others that were in the crowd: there was no waving, cheering, smiling, weeping; they didn't even appear to be straining their necks like everyone else to see the soldiers approaching. Instead they were in deep conversation with each other – conversation that was broken only with the odd pointing at something or someone across the driveway from where they stood. They were too preoccupied with what they were discussing to see Inspector Armstrong, who was watching them from fifty yards away in the crowd opposite.

The men of the 1st Battalion marched into the grounds and its officers entered the cathedral where a short service was held in the chapel named in honour of the Regiment – Non-Commissioned Officers and men stood to attention outside. After twenty minutes the officers emerged and the battalion presented arms and prepared for its final short march to the station. The two cousins managed to catch each other's eye and with a smile and a nod, said their final goodbye.

The men disappeared down English Street and the crowds within the grounds started to disperse. Cornelius looked for the two men from Burgh but they had gone.

He wandered off back through The Abbey Gate and along Dean Tait's Lane, back to work in a world of his own, wondering what the two men were up to. He knew he was visiting the village the following week and resolved to catch up with them then.

The reason for his visit to Burgh by Sands was another invitation from his friend Reverend Richard Fraser. In the intervening months, the vicar had generated enough interest in the village to hold a ceremony and street party to commemorate the six hundredth anniversary of King Edward's death.

Cornelius joined Richard and the villagers on the marsh by the red sandstone monument that marked the spot where the king died. Scores of villagers had gathered on the baking hot July afternoon; some of them had gone to the trouble of dressing up in the costume of the day, with three or four young men looking particularly impressive dressed as Knights Templar, complete with chain mail and their distinctive white mantles with the large red cross. Armstrong found himself scanning the crowd to see if he could see the two men he had spotted a week earlier in Carlisle, but as strange as their presence was at the cathedral, their absence from a village event was equally unusual.

Richard's dog Jack sat at his master's feet and yapped incessantly. As the vicar prepared to say a few words to mark the occasion he said to Cornelius, "I don't know what it is with the wretched animal! He's normally so well behaved."

Having witnessed similar behaviour during his visit on New Year's Day, Cornelius tried to placate his friend by saying with a laugh, "It's maybe just me he has a problem with!"

"Perhaps," replied Fraser, joining in the joke, "but there's another one." He pointed to another little dog that was responding to Jack's apparent discomfort in the same way.

Cornelius looked from one to the other smiling and then realised that both dogs were looking away from the monument and appeared to be attracted by something else. His gaze followed the direction of their excitement but saw nothing other than the crowd of people who were chatting and joking with one another. As Armstrong ran his eye along the crowd, he saw Richard's housekeeper, Mrs. Hunter and her husband Sam; and he recognised Michael Turner who was also there, apparently with his family; something made him then jerk his head back in sharp double-take. A particular member of the crowd looked completely incongruous with his fellow villagers: he stood at the back of the crowd, clearly a tall man, as Armstrong could see the bare headed individual through the fidgeting horde, many of whose number wore hats and bonnets. The man was staring directly at Cornelius, as if oblivious to everyone around him. The policeman appeared momentarily paralysed, rooted to the spot on which he stood; the noise from the boisterous crowd faded and the warm shafts of sunlight disappeared as the man's fiery eyes pierced right through him. Cornelius felt discomfort on his neck and shoulders and he gave an involuntary shiver.

"My dear Cornelius, are you alright?" asked Richard who stood beside him.

Armstrong became aware of the crowd and the temperature once more. "Yes ... Yes, I'm fine, thank you." After several seconds of looking at his friend, he turned back and risked another encounter but the man was gone. Cornelius scanned the crowd with some intensity but there was no sign of the fear-provoking figure. That was it, he realised: he had actually been frightened by the attention of the man!

"Are you sure you are alright, Cornelius?" asked the vicar again.

"Yes really, Richard – thank you," he said removing his hat and drawing a handkerchief over his brow. "It must be the heat."

Jack and the other dog sat with their ears down whimpering.

After regaining his composure, Cornelius asked, "Tell me Richard, where are those two other men from the study group?"

"Tom and Bill? I'm not sure," said Fraser standing on tiptoe and oscillating his neck to get a better view of those present, "I must say they have been a little withdrawn lately. I'm not sure what is wrong with them."

"Do they have any friends or relatives in the Border Regiment?"

Richard broke off his inspection of those present and sank back down onto his heels to look directly at Armstrong. "What a strange question," he said. "Not that I know of – why?"

"It's just I was down at the cathedral last week to witness the 1st Battalion leaving and I saw them there. I thought it rather unusual that's all."

"I'm not sure," said the vicar, "I suppose it does seem a little unusual. Perhaps they were in Carlisle for some other reason and simply decided to take in the parade?"

"Perhaps," said the detective, less than convinced.

The crowd finally settled and Reverend Fraser said a few words in honour of the occasion and ended by asking for God's blessing and forgiveness "...to all here present and to those who have passed through our village."

155

A collective "Amen" ended the ceremony and allowed the villagers to turn their attention to the street party that had been arranged for everyone. As they wandered in random fashion back towards the main street, Cornelius – who brought up the rear with Richard – could not resist looking over his shoulder at the monument. There was nothing, or no one, to be seen.

Chapter Eleven

Balliol's Treasure

Six hundred years earlier to the day, the body of King Edward was taken from that very spot on the marsh and moved to the parish church. As it was being laid out, wrapped in the King's long red cloak, one of his subjects found his mind racing towards other matters.

Simon Ashbourne was a slippery opportunist who had sought to curry extra favour with Edward, since the death of his master and the King's Treasurer, Rodger de Coventry three years earlier. Now that the king was also dead and there would be the inevitable hiatus between his death and the Prince of Wales's proclamation, Ashbourne knew he had to think fast and be decisive.

For ten years he had noted the various pots of treasures that Coventry had concealed away on the King's behalf: in Snowdonia and Anglesey; in Gloucester and Lincoln Cathedrals; the jewels of Gascony regained following the treaty with Philippe; the chests of silver taken in taxes from the Barons and held in the depths of Marlborough Castle; and most significantly of all, the box offered to the king by Robert the Bruce that Ashbourne remembered was held in the crypt of Carlisle Cathedral. His devious mind also recalled the Burgess of the Cathedral, William Hartley and his feelings of betrayal at being overlooked by the King for positions of higher authority.

Ashbourne quickly made his mind up and rushed back to the city to seek out Hartley; he found him in The Chapter House in the grounds of the Cathedral.

"Master Hartley, have you heard about the King's death?"

"Of course," replied the Burgess, "before the day was completed, the message was carried around the city."

There was a prolonged silence between the two, as if they both knew what each other was thinking but each was too afraid to articulate their thoughts. Finally it was Ashbourne that broached the most delicate of subjects.

"Opportunities arise every once in a while, Burgess – I believe now we have such an opportunity."

"What do you mean, Master Ashbourne?"

Ashbourne decided the time for playing games was over. "You know what I mean, Hartley. The King is dead; his son is not half the man his father was and probably does not know anything about the treasures his father had hidden away over the years. It is people like you and me who deserve their just rewards for serving a King who did not recognise our loyalty. This is our opportunity to take those rewards."

"What do you have in mind?" asked Hartley, knowing full well what the courtier was suggesting.

"If I remember correctly, the crypt is full of treasure; if we work together we could share some of those riches without the new King ever knowing."

"Already extra guards are being sent to Carlisle to guard the King's body and prepare for his son's arrival from Scotland."

Ashbourne noted that Hartley was not disagreeing with his suggestion, but merely pointing out one of the potential obstacles. "All the more reason to move quickly Master Hartley."

Hartley remained troubled. "What you are suggesting is theft; theft from the King. It is treason."

"And what have you ever received from the King?" asked Ashbourne, playing on Hartley's sense of injustice at events long since passed.

There was another prolonged silence.

Finally Hartley confirmed his acquiescence by meeting Ashbourne's stare with his own avaricious eyes. "Very well," he said, "I know a way." Ashbourne could barely contain his excitement. The Burgess continued, "We could never take anything from the treasure room and walk out of the cathedral and the city without being seen. But there is an unused drainage system deep below the ground that runs from the Nave diagonally towards the Western Wall, where there is an outlet into the town dyke. I know this drain can be accessed through a hatch in the treasure room – there are similar accesses under each of the buildings within he Abbey, where small cellars were used to maintain the tunnels."

"Why are they no longer used?" asked Ashbourne.

"Some of the tunnels which date back to the times of the Blackfriars became unstable some years ago and in some cases, there were instances of parts collapsing."

"Such a venture as ours should not be without risk," said Ashbourne after some thought, "but clearly we cannot carry a lot on such a treacherous journey."

"If you recall, Master Ashbourne, ten years ago we deposited the small chest given to the King by Bruce. Inside were bags of silver coins and details of where John Balliol had hidden his fortunes in Galloway. I know the box has remained untouched since the day we placed it there. Very few others know it is there and in the distraction caused by the King's death, I cannot believe that anyone will think to perform an inventory of the treasure room's contents. I could have a groom have horses placed outside the Western Wall – we could make our escape to Scotland and using the maps and documents, secure Balliol's treasure."

"That is an excellent plan, Master Hartley. But we will have to move quickly. I propose we go tonight."

"Tonight?" exclaimed the Burgess.

Ashbourne feared that his conspirator was in danger of stepping back from the brink, after realising the gravity of what the two men were plotting. "Hartley, we have no time to lose. You said yourself that the King's army will return with his body from Burgh in the next day; then the Prince will arrive from Scotland with *his* army. Carlisle will be the most fortified city in Christendom within two days – if we do not move now, our chance will be lost."

"Very well," said Hartley with some reluctance. "I am always the last person in the Cathedral after dark. The final vigil finishes at the hour of ten – be here after that."

Ashbourne left the Chapter House knowing that this was the chance he had been waiting for after many a long year. He knew that the new King Edward II did not have his father's skill to inspire his men and strike fear into his enemies; the Scottish campaigns were bound to fail as a result. Furthermore, there would be no place for him in the new court, so if he could find himself on the other side of the Border within days, as the new king was making the reverse journey to pay homage to his father, then he could pursue Balliol's treasure in virtual anonymity.

At the appointed hour, under a black sky, he met William Hartley at the door of Carlisle Cathedral. The two shadows entered the empty church and the Burgess led the way with a small candle down to the crypt. Ashbourne remembered the journey the two had made some ten years earlier; his heart beat faster on this occasion as he prepared to commit a crime from which there was no going back.

Hartley crossed the crypt and opened the door to the treasury. He then locked the door behind them and lit two of the long wall mounted torches. It was exactly how Ashbourne had remembered it; his eye fell on the chest given to the King in 1297.

"Can we open it?" he asked.

"It has the King's seal on it but if we are to steal it I do not suppose it will make much difference," replied Hartley.

Ashbourne took his dagger from its scabbard and levered the clasp of the chest. Hartley took one of the torches down and held it over the open box. Inside were the bags of coins offered to the king by Bruce on behalf of his father and underneath were a selection of documents that – as far as the two men could establish – referred to locations within

Galloway where King John Balliol had secreted his riches, much as Edward had done throughout his own Kingdom.

"We are rich, Master Hartley," said Ashbourne, greedily peering into the box.

Hartley knelt down and seemed to hesitate – his treachery was now becoming very real; his confederate sensed it.

"It is no time to lose our nerve now," he said, cajoling his fellow conspirator into action.

Hartley was paralysed with fear, "I am not sure, Ashbourne, this is not right." He held up his torch as he spoke to Ashbourne; the light created a giant shadow against the cellar wall behind the tall man, giving him a fearsome appearance.

"What have you to remain in Carlisle for?" said the King's Courtier grabbing Hartley's arm. "Do you think you will achieve any more recognition under the new King Edward than the old one? You have no family here – this is your one chance to finally get what you deserve after all of your years of loyal service."

Hartley moved his torch and shone it towards the far wall of the treasury. At its base was a large slab with an iron ring set in its middle. "Very well," he said, "we can access the old drainage tunnel through there."

Chapter Twelve

The Cost of Avarice

Beyond the trap door, the yawning black hole became a dank menacing environment; five smooth looking, slippery stones led down into the derelict drainage channel. Ashbourne led the way with the small chest under one arm and the long torch at the end of the other; his nervous and doubtful companion took some coaxing down the steps behind him.

"Come on, Master Hartley, there is little time to waste."

Hartley reluctantly followed and stepped into the ankle-deep water that lay stagnant in the base of the long cylindrical tunnel that stretched into the darkness. He held up his torch and saw the brick wall glistening back at him; he then looked down with disgust to see his cloak trailing in the scummy liquid and felt the horrible wetness between his toes as it soaked through his sandals and thick woolen socks.

"*Come on*, Hartley!" demanded Ashbourne who, despite his tall frame, was now many yards ahead of the Burgess. As he pressed on, Ashbourne realised that Hartley had served his purpose; he now had the chest with the maps – if Hartley chose to follow, that was his affair; if not, then he could easily press on himself.

Hartley continued tentatively, in a crouched shuffle along the cramped tunnel. He saw the torch of his companion ahead but struggled to take his eyes from the black pock marks in the cylindrical corridor where bricks had been dislodged from the poorly constructed tunnel; whenever he saw the holes, his gaze instantly fell to the base of the tunnel where the fallen bricks lay in the stagnant water. He looked up ahead again and was aghast to see two or three bricks fall and splash into the water in front of him; clearly the slight juddering caused by Ashbourne's progress was enough to destabilise the bricks that appeared in places to be wedged together without any mortar.

"Ashbourne!" Hartley's call was a whispered shout. Ashbourne apparently didn't hear and bundled on, now some fifty paces in front. Again Hartley saw bricks fall between himself and Ashbourne. He was now losing his nerve completely, *"ASHBOURNE! ASHBOURNE!"* The king's courtier started, as Hartley's shout echoed up the tunnel; he half turned and half stumbled, forcing him down onto one knee. The vibration of his fall was enough for the area directly above him to give way completely: dozens of bricks followed by mounds of earth came crashing down into the base of the drainage channel.

In blind panic, Ashbourne managed to leap further along the tunnel and away from the collapse – to his further fright, he found himself falling from a ledge in the blackness onto the floor of what appeared to be a small chamber. Having lost his grip on both the small chest and the torch – which had been extinguished in the kafuffle – Ashbourne knelt in the total blackness as the air thickened with the dust and debris that poured into the tiny room from the collapse. Momentarily he felt relief at the near miss, but then he felt his way around the underground compartment and realised there was no way out! The direction in which he was travelling – towards the Western Wall – had been bricked up and obviously the direction from which he came was now blocked by a mass of soil and rubble. Relief gave way to fear.

"HARTLEY! HARTLEY!" he screamed as loud as he could.

Hartley had witnessed the tunnel collapse in horror from further back, and thought at that point it had fallen on top of Ashbourne. He scampered along towards the cave-in not knowing what he could do, but compelled to help his companion. He heard Ashbourne's screams for help and thought there may be a chance to free him; he stood his torch upright about ten paces behind him so as not to risk losing its light, and started clawing at the mound of debris with his bare hands, "I'm here, Ashbourne!" he called.

As he feverishly dug, some more bricks started to dislodge from their housing above – one struck him on the head causing him to leap back in anger. He stood in silence – the air thick with choking, peaty dust – trying to focus on the damaged tunnel walls in the dim light and wondering how stable the remainder of the construction was. He decided to go back and pick up the torch that would at least give him a better view. He had barely retreated three paces when he halted at the sound of a terrifying creaking noise above him – he instinctively quickened his pace and almost simultaneously, the spot where he stood a second earlier became covered as another part of the tunnel collapsed. The vibration caused the torch that stood upright against the tunnel wall to topple over and its open flame fizzled into nothingness as it fell into the slimy liquid base.

Hartley was now completely in the dark but knew that the instability of the drainage channel made any attempt to rescue Ashbourne impossible; his only course of action now was to get out of this black hell. He scuttled along back in the direction from which they came; he tripped on his sodden cloak and lost his footing; trying to get back to his feet, his leather sandals slipped on the wet base. Panic was threatening to overtake him.

He glanced behind into the darkness – he could not see anything; the tunnel creaked and moaned as if shooing him away. More bricks fell; obviously the dislodging of one was causing the weakening of the next and this knock-on effect would inevitably lead to a total complete collapse.

Hartley finally saw the five steps ahead of him; their slippery surface glistened with the tiny amount of light that was thrown upon them by the torches in the treasury. He managed to scramble up the steps and onto the stone floor where he lay on his back panting. All of a sudden there was an almighty crash beneath him as the drainage channel finally collapsed completely in on itself. A plume of black dust threatened to engulf the treasury through the hatch, but Hartley managed to lift the small stone trap door back into place and seal whatever damage there was below ground. It was only then that he remembered that Simon Ashbourne was also trapped down there with no means of escape; Hartley had been his only hope and he had deserted him.

The Burgess sat in complete silence. The dimly lit treasury – a room he once guarded with pride and enthusiasm – now seemed like his own, personal dungeon. He wept.

The feelings of injustice that led him into this stupidity in the first place; the guilt he now felt after leaving Ashbourne to his fate; the thought of being branded a common criminal; his reputation in tatters. All these feelings and the sudden realisation of his folly welled up in him to create an overwhelming feeling of self-loathing.

He quite deliberately got up, locked the doors of the treasury and the crypt behind him; walked the length of the cathedral to the opening that led to the spiral stone steps, to the left of the altar. Along the top of the gantry he walked in the darkness towards the bell tower, a journey he had made a thousand times or more previously. This was to be the last.

Once he was high in the bell chamber itself, he reached down awkwardly under one of the bells and heaved up its large rope to create some slack on the platform on which he stood. With great difficulty he held the weight of the rope – which was as thick as his wrist – with one hand, while he wrapped the slack around his own neck three times with the other. As soon as he let go, the weight of the rope fell and ripped him off the platform, snapping his neck in the process and leaving him dangling under the tolling bell.

Chapter Thirteen

Arson Attack

It was a late September afternoon when Cornelius Armstrong's train pulled into Carlisle station. He had spent the last two days on a seminar for Detective Inspectors that were held from time to time in Preston. Armstrong was more of a home-bird and not by nature a gregarious creature, and was never in a rush to attend; once there however, he found the camaraderie of his colleagues quite enjoyable. The previous evening he had enjoyed spending a couple of hours in the pub with his colleague Daniel Standish; both men had helped each other professionally on more than one occasion in the past. All in all, Cornelius concluded that a change was indeed as good as a rest.

The train breathed heavily and prepared for the final leg of its journey to Glasgow, as Cornelius and his fellow passengers walked along the platform and out into the afternoon sunlight. As he walked across the square, through the twin rotunda and onto English Street, he heard the familiar high pitched cry of the two young urchins who, each afternoon, stood outside the gaol, selling newspapers from behind a billboard that proclaimed the latest local news. It wasn't until Armstrong was virtually at their stand when he made out what today's proclamation was.

"*Fire at the Cathedral!*" shouted one of the boys as loud as he could.

"*Arson suspected!*" yelled the other.

"When did this happen?" questioned the policeman.

"Last night, sir," said one of the boys, offering him a newspaper.

"What damage is there?" said Cornelius, reaching in his pocket for some change.

"One of the buildings has gone, sir."

"And who said it was arson," asked the detective, completing the purchase.

The two boys looked at one another. "I dunno sir," said one, "we dunno what arson is – the boss just telt us to shout it!"

Armstrong looked at the pitiful creatures before him: rotting teeth and large welts on their bare feet; their cheeks sunken with consumption and malnutrition gave more than enough evidence of the difficulties endured by such children. The detective thanked the boys, added a little tip for them and hurried along English Street. He now suspected that his day – that he had thought was coming to an end – was only just beginning.

Hastening through the gates of the Cathedral, the realisation of what had happened came as a mix of shock and relief: the church itself appeared undamaged by the fire, but the large detached house that stood within the Abbey and diagonally opposite the front door of the Cathedral was clearly gutted. The front door and all of the windows at the front of the house were gone, as was the roof. Despite it presumably being twelve or more hours since the blaze, the interior still smoldered and pale wisps of smoke could be seen in the afternoon sun, eddying their way skyward through the non-existent roof.

Two uniformed officers were guarding the stricken building and instinctively stood to attention when they saw their superior coming through the gate at a half-run.

"Afternoon, sir," said Joe Brady. He and Harry Stokes both touched the brims of their helmets in acknowledgement.

"When did this happen?" asked Armstrong.

"Through the night, sometime, sir," said Brady. "The alarm was raised around five o'clock this morning."

"Was anybody inside?"

"No, sir, as luck would have it, the house was empty."

"Was it started deliberately?"

"We think so, sir – someone was seen running down Abbey Street by the same person who raised the alarm."

Armstrong asked Stokes to take his bag the short distance to his lodgings; as the Police Constable walked away, the Inspector moved towards the building. The fire had been so intense that the only thing left was the four walls that formed the outer shell. He placed the palms of his hands on either side of the front doorway and leant in – the sickening smell of the fire's aftermath filled his nostrils. Beyond the threshold of the doorway, there was a three-foot drop to a thick carpet of light grey smoldering ash.

"There seems to have been a timber floor, sir," said Brady from over his shoulder, "it's obviously gone now to reveal the sub floor underneath. We haven't been able to get in yet because the ash is still hot. It must have been some blaze."

"You said there was a witness?"

"Well, not a witness as such, sir, but someone saw somebody running away. This is the same bloke who raised the alarm – he lives over there in the end house." Brady gestured with his chin towards the row of three terrace houses at the north end of the Cathedral grounds beside the Abbey Gate.

Armstrong followed his indication. "Have we spoken to him yet?"

"Sergeant Smith spoke to him earlier, sir. Seems like a bit of a snooty so-and-so if you ask me."

"Well there's not much more we can do here till the morning, I suppose," said the Inspector as PC Stokes re-appeared through the Abbey Gate. "You and Harry keep watch here and I'll go and have a chat with...what's his name?"

Brady unbuttoned his top pocket, took out his notebook and flicked over the pages. "Williams, sir," he said, apparently struggling to read his own writing, "...Joseph Williams."

Inspector Armstrong walked over, wrapped firmly on the door and waited. He noticed out of the corner of his eye that the net curtains at the downstairs window twitched; rustling noises emanated from inside before, after about a minute, the door was snatched open, revealing a tall man of around sixty with a high forehead and a long nose.

"Yes?" he said haughtily.

Cornelius instantly recognised the Cathedral official: often seen around the Abbey and if memory served, the rather obnoxious individual who had given him short shrift before the service on Christmas Day.

"Mr. Williams?"

Williams seemed to know he was being addressed by a policeman; Cornelius was under the impression that had this not been the case, he wouldn't have answered at all.

"Yes," he said at last.

The detective decided against messing about with the preliminaries – Williams knew what he wanted. "My name is Inspector Cornelius Armstrong – I believe you saw someone running away from the scene of the fire this morning?"

"I told your colleague everything I know earlier today," said Williams dismissively.

"Well now you can tell me," replied Armstrong adopting a stricter tone.

Williams realised that the policeman wasn't intending to take 'no' for an answer. He rolled his eyes and exhaled loudly before beginning his narrative. "At about five o'clock this morning, my wife shook me awake and said she had heard something in the Abbey. I put on my dressing gown and slippers and came down stairs. As I did so, I heard someone running past the front of the house and through the Abbey Gate. I looked through the curtains but couldn't see anything – it was then that I ventured outside. The side door of the Abbey Gate was open and I could see a man through it running down Abbey Street. At that same moment that I realised the Head Verger's house was on fire."

"Can you describe the man you saw?" asked Armstrong.

170

"No I cannot. He was some distance from me and was running away. He was dressed in black and it was still dark."

"The Head Verger's house you say. I believe he wasn't there last night?"

"He is staying with Reverend Hope at St Cuthbert's. He had vacated his house yesterday morning as it was due to be decorated over the next few days. Will there be anything else?" asked Williams curtly.

"No, I think that will be all, Mr. Williams – *for now*'" Cornelius couldn't resist adding extra inflection to the end of his sentence, knowing the irritation it would cause. Williams responded with another roll of the eyes and a closing of the door without further pleasantry.

Armstrong decided to go to the station and find out what his Detective Sergeant had discovered.

"Where's Sergeant Smith?" he asked the Duty Sergeant as he entered.

"He's gone home, sir," replied Bill Townsend, a little sheepishly, "he's had a long day with being called out early."

Armstrong reached into his pocket and flicked open his watch: gone six. "I suppose time is getting on," he said, half to himself. "You get yourself away an' all, Bill – I'll lock up later."

"Thank you, sir," said the sergeant grabbing his coat.

Cornelius glanced through the papers on Sergeant Smith's desk; there didn't appear to be anything other than what he had found out from Williams earlier. While he was at the station – and in order to give himself a fresh start in the morning – he decided to catch up on the paperwork that had accumulated during his two-day absence.

His train had arrived at four o'clock, but it was after eleven by the time Cornelius finally entered his lodgings on Abbey Street. He was met by his ever dependable housekeeper.

"Have y'ad anything to eat, Mr. Armstrong?" she asked as he entered.

"I managed to get a sandwich earlier, thank you, Mrs. Wheeler. I think I'll just turn in."

"Whadthecawme – that's a queer carry on at the Cathedral isn't it?" said Mrs. Wheeler as her lodger started to climb the stairs.

"It is I'm afraid," agreed the policeman.

"Aye, nothing's sacred nowadays," said Isabella as she pulled her shawl over her shoulders and started towards the basement of her house.

"I think I'm in for a busy day tomorrow," said Cornelius, prior to them wishing each other goodnight.

Chapter Fourteen

Reverend Fraser's Discomfort

Cornelius climbed into bed at around half past eleven. Around the same time, about seven miles away at the Old Vicarage in Burgh by Sands, Reverend Richard Fraser did exactly the same thing. The last two days had proved more than a little disconcerting for the Vicar of St Michael's and he was now looking forward to a less traumatic night's sleep.

The previous morning, the day had begun in a regular fashion that saw him make a few pastoral calls to parishioners in and around the village. After a light lunch, it was off to the station to catch the two o'clock train into Carlisle. The purpose of his visit was to fulfil an invitation to St Cuthbert's from his friend the Reverend Edmund Hope, who was hosting George Hammond, the Head Verger from the Cathedral. Edmund decided it would be an ideal opportunity to also ask Richard and the Reverend Nicholas Stuart from the Cathedral to join them for dinner and a general catch-up.

Not surprisingly, Reverend Fraser came across Michael Turner going about his duties at the station when he arrived a few minutes before two o'clock. Turner was standing on the platform talking to Tom Carmichael who had apparently called on his friend to drop in a recipe on behalf of his wife for Mrs. Turner.

"Good afternoon, gentlemen," said Richard as he climbed onto the platform.

"Reverend!" said Turner, "what are you doing going to the 'big smoke'?"

"Oh, I've just had an invitation from my friend at St Cuthbert's to spend the evening with him and his guests."

"Big party is it?" chipped in Carmichael, teasing the vicar.

"Hardly," said the vicar laughing, "I'm joining a couple of colleagues from the Cathedral for a quiet dinner."

"The Cathedral?" repeated Carmichael.

"Yes, the Head Verger is staying there while his house is being decorated and – "

"Who, sorry?" interrupted Carmichael who was now listening intently after hitherto, only being mildly interested and amused by the exchange.

"George Hammond, the Head Verger – his is the large detached house that stands across from the main entrance. Apparently they are going to decorate all of the properties within the Abbey and his is the first. I think – "

For the second time, Carmichael interrupted the Reverend, "Er, sorry, gentlemen, I've just remembered I had to meet my wife at two o'clock. He hurried off, shouting over his shoulder, 'I'll see you both later."

The two men stood looking at one another, bemused by the apparent rudeness of their friend. Their confusion was interrupted by the arrival of the train; Fraser boarded with a slightly more polite farewell exchange with Turner and went on his way.

But an uncomfortable day followed for the Reverend Fraser; of course, he enjoyed the company of his friends; he enjoyed the change that a trip to the city brought – a very different experience from that of the quiet village life; and he enjoyed the fine meal, prepared by Reverend Hope's housekeeper at St Cuthbert's Vicarage. But throughout the day he could not shake off an inexplicable feeling of foreboding.

He returned to Burgh on the ten o'clock train and spent a restive night. The following morning appeared to confirm Richard's feelings of discomfort when news of a fire at the Cathedral reached the village. He rushed back to Carlisle to see if he could be of any assistance, only to find that the damage to the Head Verger's house was horrendous and nothing could done to salvage the building or its contents. Its occupant, George Hammond was naturally in a distressed state; it was clear that his stay at St Cuthbert's – originally scheduled to be a few days – was now likely to be several months. By six o'clock that evening it was obvious to Richard that his presence was starting to become more of a hindrance than a help; he therefore repeated his journey home from the previous night.

Less than an hour later, as the village gradually succumbed to the fading light, he was approaching St Michael's once more. His housekeeper, Mrs. Hunter, had long since finished her duties, so it was left to Richard to have a final check around the grounds and lock the church up for the night.

As was his custom he went into the church and knelt in one of the forward pews for a little reflection. For the first time in the months he had been at St Michael's, he felt a certain discomfort: he almost sensed a presence – not of God but something almost malevolent.

Unable to settle into his prayer, he rose and crept carefully around the dimly-lit church. The flames of the candles on the altar and the side aisles seemed to fidget uncomfortably, and created tiny dancing shadows on the stone walls. The deep, black recesses and the alcoves of the church maintained their eerie stillness. Fraser suddenly spun round as – out of the corner of his eye – he saw one of the guttering candles on the altar finally breathe its last; a tiny strand of smoke floated upward and dissipated into the darkness. He decided that this traumatic day was now playing tricks on him and it was time to bring it to a close. He blew out the remaining candles and locked the church door behind him, giving the latch a sturdy rattle to ensure its security.

The ever-reliable Mrs. Hunter had prepared a cold supper for the returning vicar, which he enjoyed enormously. He then spent a few hours reading in his study before going to bed shortly before eleven o'clock. The Reverend tossed and turned for some time until he dropped off "...well after midnight," as he later recalled and fell into a deep sleep. In what seemed to him like an instant later he leapt in his bed, as he was jolted back to consciousness with a violent start – *the church bell was ringing!*

Two enormous clangs of the bell were followed by a third ring that was considerably quieter. Richard's heart lurched in fear and shock. He went to his window and peered out to see if there was anything obvious; he thought he saw something move in the shadows. Gathering his senses after a few minutes, he wrapped himself in his dressing gown, ventured downstairs and opened the front door. For the second time in the space of ten minutes, he leapt in fright as he was greeted by the large figure of PC Sam Phillips, the village 'Bobby', who lived in the closest dwelling to the church, and who was also awakened by the bell. Phillips also leapt back as Fraser snatched open the door from the unlit hallway.

"Reverend!" said Phillips with a mixture of shock and relief, "I heard the bell and wondered what was going on."

"Sam!" exclaimed Fraser, with a mock hand gesture to his chest, "am I pleased to see you?! I thought I was dreaming until the bell sounded again."

Phillips had obviously rushed out of the house quickly as his trousers and braces were pulled over his night shirt. "How did it ring?" he asked, unsure whether he was being obtuse or not.

"I don't know," replied the equally confused vicar.

The two stepped out from the house and went round to the front of the church to investigate. Looking up, they saw the bats wheeling around the bell tower, clearly disturbed from their roost; their screeching was swallowed up by the silence of the dark night. It was too dark for the two men to see anything through the small apertures of the bell tower, so Fraser tentatively moved towards the main door of the church – he later recalled that, had it not been for the presence of PC Phillips, he was unsure as to whether or not he would have mustered up the courage. He grabbed the latch of the door and tugged: it was locked. He yanked harder so the whole of the large timber door juddered in its frame but clearly the door had not been disturbed.

"Is there any other way into the church, or up to the tower?" Phillips's question clutched at straws as he already knew the answer.

"None," replied Fraser anyway.

"Could it have been a gust of wind?" Phillips's voice tailed off as he realised the stupidity of his question on such a still night. Fraser didn't bother answering.

After standing in the darkness for a few more minutes, Phillips made a suggestion. "There is nothing we can do now. Why don't we wait until morning and then look into it? There's probably an innocent explanation for all this."

"I suppose you're right," said Richard.

Clearly neither man had an appetite for investigating further, and the two went their separate ways. Back in his room, Richard sat on his bed – he lifted his hand and realised it was trembling with fear. He went over to the washing bowl and splashed some water on his sweating brow. He lay awake for some hours listening with a certain apprehension, but all he could hear was the rapid thumping of his heart.

Chapter Fifteen

The Gruesome Discovery

Cornelius Armstrong had the almost smug feeling of the policeman about to embark on a major case. Although he was appalled by the apparent arson attack at the Cathedral, it represented his first significant investigation of the year to date. Little did he know as he walked the short distance to the station, that the case would unravel itself to be far more than a random case of arson. Even more incredible, Armstrong could never have predicted that he would have it solved before the day was out.

He had barely been sitting at his desk for ten minutes when Sergeant Townsend came through to his office and informed him of "... an urgent telephone call." Armstrong followed the Duty Sergeant through to the entrance area and picked up the candlestick telephone.

"Hello, Inspector Armstrong speaking."

"Cornelius, it's Richard."

Armstrong initially couldn't make out the voice that crackled over the line. "Richard?"

"Richard...Fraser, from St Michael's."

"*Oh, Richard!* I'm so sorry, I didn't recog–"

"Cornelius, you must come at once. Something terrible has happened!"

Within an hour, Inspector Armstrong was at the Old Vicarage at Burgh by Sands once more, this time with two uniformed colleagues. He was greeted on the step by Mrs. Hunter. "He's in the study, sir. Go right through."

179

As he entered the Reverend's study, he saw Fraser sitting at an angle with his face partially obscured by the wings of his large chair. It was only when the policeman entered and walked round to greet him that he grasped the arms of the chair and attempted to haul himself up. Armstrong saw his ashen complexion and helped him back down.

"Sit down, Richard. You've had a terrible shock."

Fraser had briefly given Armstrong the tragic and shocking news earlier on the telephone; news that prompted the Detective Inspector to rush out to Burgh once more. Now he went through the events of the last few hours in greater detail. He began by recounting the strange events of the previous night: the bell, his search with PC Phillips and his feelings of discomfort.

"I must confess the first light of dawn brought with it a deep sense of relief. I had slept fitfully as you might imagine, but as those orange rays streamed into my room, somehow my whole body relaxed from the tension it had been under all night." Fraser stared blankly into the fire. "It was almost as though the sunlight provided the assurance that, for the time being at least, the danger from the previous night was over." Richard seemed to snap out of his reverie and continued with more purpose.

"Mrs. Hunter arrived around half past seven, just as I was coming down the stairs. 'PC Phillips is outside, Reverend,' she said, 'I think there is something wrong with the bell tower.'

"I went outside to see Phillips looking up. 'Morning, Reverend, there's certainly something up there.'

"I looked up. There was a curious deep background sighing as the wind passed through the apertures and caressed the huge iron bell. But it was not that that was attracting the attention of Phillips: something appeared to be draped down the outside of the bell that caused it to sit at an unnatural angle. Because the apertures are relatively small, it was difficult to make out exactly what it was at this stage. I retrieved the key from to the church and Phillips and I went in."

The two men found the church cold and dark but that was not unusual at that time of morning. In the far corner of the church was the narrow, stone, spiral staircase that led to the bell tower. Reverend Fraser began to climb it first; Sam Phillips following him. Repeatedly banging his head and shoulders against the stone walls as he became increasingly disoriented, Phillips maneuvered his bulky frame up the tiny steps that seemed to get narrower the higher they climbed, until they gave the illusion of instantly twisting back on themselves. As he ascended, the policeman clung on to the large rope that was fixed to the wall of the staircase with iron cleats, and acted as a handrail.

Finally Phillips reached the timber floor of the tower from where the bell was rung and maintained; the instant he did so, he caught the Reverend as he staggered back with a shriek of horror! As he cradled the vicar and thus prevented him from falling back down the steps, Phillips looked over Fraser's shoulder at the cause of the clergyman's fright. A rope had been lashed to the top of the giant mechanism that supported the bell – dangling at the end of the rope that hung below the bell and over the dark abyss below was the lifeless body of Bill Hartley.

"And the church was locked last night?" questioned Inspector Armstrong at the conclusion of the vicar's narrative.

"Yes, I locked it myself and made sure later when Sam and I checked it when the bell ra..." It was only at this point that Richard realised that it must have been Hartley jumping to his death that disturbed the bell and caused it to ring.

"So he must have been in the church when you locked up last evening," concluded Armstrong.

Fraser thought back to his strange experience in church when he sensed someone's presence. He put his head in his hands and sobbed bitterly. "The poor man, if only–"

"Don't blame yourself, Richard," consoled Cornelius, "no one could have predicted this. I suggest we go and take him down. You can stay here if you like – there is no need to further distress yourself."

"No, I need to be there, Cornelius," Fraser's tone was stoic, "the village will need its vicar at a time like this. I need to pull myself together."

Armstrong mustered his two men and, together with PC Phillips, he and Fraser made their way round to the church and up the precarious assent, full in the knowledge that a grisly discovery awaited them. Once on the timber platform, Armstrong took out his pocket book and made some notes of the scene before him. PC Sam Phillips corroborated Richard Fraser's version of the events and the Inspector gave the order to his men and Phillips to take the body down.

As he did so, the group became aware of a commotion at the foot of the steps below them. "Reverend?" cried a voice. "Inspector Armstrong? Could you come down please?"

When they appeared through the small opening at the foot of the steps, they saw Mrs. Hunter who obviously knew what the men were doing, having been present earlier that morning when Fraser and Phillips had discovered Hartley's body. No one else in the village knew of the tragedy and Fraser – knowing that the small community would be shocked and stunned by the suicide – had assured Armstrong that one of Mrs. Hunter's greatest virtues was her discretion. It was not however, about Hartley's suicide that Mrs. Hunter wanted to speak with Fraser and Armstrong.

"I'm sorry to trouble you gentlemen, but Sissy Carmichael's man has gone missing!"

"Tom?" said the vicar.

"Yes sir. Never come home last night apparently. I've just had her round at the vicarage – in a terrible state she is. I've sent her home and said I would send a policeman round to see her."

"Whatever next?" asked Richard despairingly.

Armstrong had left the three uniformed officers with the delicate task of taking down the body, so suggested that he would go and see Mrs. Carmichael himself. Richard offered to accompany him.

They found her in a highly agitated state; she sat on the edge of a wooden stool in her austere kitchen, rocking back and forward, and ringing her hands. Armstrong questioned her as delicately as he could.

How long had her husband been missing? It seems as though he'd been gone for two nights. Mrs. Carmichael had been looking after her sick sister at Moorehouse for two days; when she came home there was no sign that their bed had been slept in. Was there any note from her husband? None. Had he been acting strangely recently? Mrs. Carmichael said he had not but Richard Fraser could not help thinking about the odd encounter he had on the station platform. He thought it best not to raise this in front of the man's wife however.

Armstrong tried to assuage the woman as best he could by assuring her that he would look into the matter. The two men went to show themselves out. As they did so, Cornelius noticed two books lying on a dresser that stood under the front window: one concerned Edward I's time in Carlisle, and the second was a tatty, dullish-green book that turned out to be a history of the Cathedral. Armstrong paused for a moment and picked it up and it virtually fell open at a page that had its top right hand corner turned down; the page itself referred to the old drainage system that ran under the Cathedral. Cornelius had a flashback moment and remembered that this was the book Carmichael was carrying under his arm the day he had the chance encounter with him and Hartley at the library in May.

"Are you coming, Cornelius?" asked Richard with his hand on the door latch.

"What? Oh yes of course. Sorry."

The two returned to the church where the policemen had brought Bill Hartley's body down from the bell tower. Armstrong peered down on it as it lay on the cold stone at the back of the church. The face had a bluish hue and the raw mark around the neck made a cause of death diagnosis simple to the most amateurish of pathologists. Armstrong's eye then drifted to his clothes: under Hartley's outer coat, his once white shirt was blackened with sweat and...*soot!* The policeman knelt down and grabbed a handful of Hartley's coat – there was a distinct smell of smoke matted in the fabric. Instantly, everything fell into place in the policeman's mind.

"What is it?" asked the Reverend Fraser, who stood above the Inspector, along with the three uniformed policemen.

"I'm afraid, Richard, it is the worst possible news. If I am right you need to prepare yourself for another shock – something that will shake this village to its very core." Then, walking towards the door, he added, "I need to use your telephone as a matter of urgency."

Chapter Sixteen

Tragedy Strikes

The final thirty-six hours of Bill Hartley's life began with his friend Tom Carmichael running breathlessly into the yard, where Hartley tended to his employer's horse, shortly after two o'clock.

"*Bill, Bill* – I've just heard from the Reverend that the house we've been talking about at the Cathedral is empty for a few days. This is our chance to find out what's under there!"

It had been some weeks since Hartley had done any further investigation in to the subject and he found his appetite for the search starting to wane somewhat. "I don't know, Tom," he said with a less than enthusiastic grimace, "it seems a bit fanciful that something would be down there after all these years."

Carmichael had always been the driving force behind the two men's subversive investigations and he wasn't about to give up now: his wife was away for a couple of days; Hartley lived on his own and had no one to miss him for the night; and the focus of their attention for many a long month – the Head Verger's house in the Cathedral grounds – was now standing empty. He was not about to give up this golden opportunity of possibly finding Balliol's maps, that would lead to riches just a few miles over the Scottish Border. He made a compelling argument and persevered with his friend until he convinced him to go along with the plan. 'The worst that can happen is that we find nothing and go without a night's sleep. At least our curiosity will be satisfied once and for all.'

"Very well." Hartley spoke with some reluctance, and yet a feeling of obligation towards his friend prompted him to agree.

"We'll meet at eight and get the train through to Carlisle," said Tom with much exhilaration. "We can hang about the Gaol Tap till kicking-out-time."

Hartley watched thoughtfully as his friend left the yard with an excited spring in his step.

Later that night, as planned, the two blended in effortlessly with the working-class clientele of *The City Arms*, known colloquially as 'The Gaol Tap' due to the fact that it backed on to the city's prison. Even the few tools they carried in an old bass simply marked them down as a couple of railway workers coming off their shift; no one gave them a second glance.

At ten o'clock the pub disgorged its patrons who gradually dissipated to the four corners of the city. The two figures of Carmichael and Hartley however – dressed in dark workmen's coats and flat caps – had other ideas. Once the throng had dispersed, they made their way quietly down West Walls and through St Cuthbert's Churchyard, to the rear of which led through an opening in a brick wall and into the rear of the Cathedral grounds. Approaching the Head Verger's house from the unseen rear virtually guaranteed the two men anonymity in the black night. A little jemmying of the kitchen window with a crow-bar and they were in, taking great care not to knock over two paraffin lamps that stood on the window sill.

They stood for several minutes in silence to confirm that the house was indeed empty. Hartley insisted they search the property to make doubly sure; the two stealthily crept through each room before a silent nod confirmed it was time to go to work.

The house may have been empty but it was still furnished and was apparently waiting for the decorators to start work in earnest the following day as, in one of the reception rooms, a pile of painters' dust sheets were rolled up in a corner. Next to them stood half a dozen wooden trestles and some lengths of plank that were obviously to be used by the men for ceiling work.

Carmichael slowly and quietly drew the thick green baize curtains that hung in each of the two rooms. "Perfect," he whispered in the darkness, "we can use one of those paraffin lamps."

The lamp did its best to throw a soft pool of light around the room as they drew back one of the rugs to lever up the floorboards in the emptier of the two rooms. Four of the boards came up easily and Carmichael eased himself down approximately four feet between the joists, to the sub floor below.

"See anything?" asked Bill Hartley quietly, as he knelt down on the remaining floorboards and peered down into the murk.

Carmichael hunched down in the confined space and moved the lantern around to see if he could see anything obvious. The base of the floor consisted of large square, stone slabs that looked as though they hadn't been disturbed since the day the floor had been laid. Dirt, debris and builders' rubble covered the slabs but as Tom brushed the dust away to reveal the surface of each slab, his silence told his friend above that their adventure was proving futile.

"No," replied Carmichael after a while. Even he seemed to be losing some of his enthusiasm; what had started out as an exciting expedition that may end up making the two rich, was now beginning to look like a fool's errand that could potentially land them in trouble.

"What do you think then?" asked Hartley as his friend levered himself back up to ground level.

"Well, we've come this far – we might as well have a look in the other room."

In order to reduce the banging and potential for arousing attention, they decided to leave the floorboards and replace them all together later. They moved to the other room and repeated the process adopted in the first; the painters' equipment was tucked away in the corner sufficiently to allow them to carry out the subversive activity with the minimum of inconvenience.

Again, Carmichael eased his way between the joists having removed a number of floorboards and again shone the paraffin lamp around the cluttered sub-floor; again Bill Hartley watched and waited from above with baited breath.

"*Hang on a minute!*" exclaimed Tom after a while.

"What is it?" asked Hartley.

"There's a ..." Carmichael feverishly brushed away the dust and debris, "... there's a ring here!"

"A ring?"

After several seconds more of clearing the way, Tom could barely disguise his delight. "*Yes!* It's a hatch – see?" he moved out of the way so his friend could lean down through the gaps in the joists and see the small pool of light illuminate a rusted iron ring that was set into one of the large slabs.

"There has to be a cellar below here, Bill – just as we suspected."

"How are we going to get it open?"

"How do you think? Brute force and ignorance! But, where there's will there's a way."

Hartley lowered himself between the joists with some difficulty and the two set to work by the dim glow of the paraffin lamp. For over an hour they chipped away, cleaning the joints around the slab to try and encourage some movement in an object that had apparently lain undisturbed for several hundreds of years. Finally, by leaning back and grabbing the joist above them with one hand, and the large ring with the other, they managed to move it ever so slightly; it was all the encouragement they needed.

More perseverance saw them manage to wedge a couple of bricks – left by various workmen over the years – between the slab and its housing. Not only were these giant flags four feet square, Hartley and Carmichael now discovered they were some four inches thick. The one they worked on was too heavy to lift out of its housing and the fact that the joists were only four feet above them meant that they couldn't flip the heavy trap door back on itself to reveal what was beneath it. They decided therefore to continue propping the slab up bit by bit, until there was enough room to see in and climb down into the cellar below.

After a further half hour of back-breaking work in the desperately confined space, they had raised the slab about three feet, so it sat at an angle of forty-five degrees, almost touching the floor joists above; it was wedged open with a short length of two-by-two timber and as many bricks as the two men could gather together.

"This is it, Bill!" said Carmichael, as he maneuvered himself towards the mouth of the opening; but then with a sense of anti-climax he declared, "I can't see a damn thing down there – the blasted lamp is going out!"

"There was another in the kitchen," said Hartley, "I'll go and get it."

"Good idea. I'll lower myself down and you can pass me the lamp."

Hartley climbed out of the sub-floor, put his fists into the small of his back and arched himself up on to his tip-toes – his muscles screamed with fatigue. He worked his neck muscles by circling his head; the stretching felt good after what seemed like hours under floor level. He went through to the kitchen and deliberately lit the paraffin lamp. Carefully retracing his steps through the house, he heard his friends' echoing voice from below as he entered the room.

"I think there's something down here, Bill!"

In his excitement, Hartley hurried to the opening in the floor, underneath which his friend was working; but in his haste, he tripped on one of the loose floorboards and fell sprawling towards the open floor joists. The innocent accident set in motion a fatal chain reaction:

Hartley came crashing down on the three open joists; the impact of his body stimulated whatever springiness there was in the timber supports; this in turn caused the joists to make contact with the open edge of the slab, which was propped up at an angle less than an inch below them. The slight disturbance was all the encouragement the large heavy flag needed to split the piece of wood and few bricks that held it open; it slammed shut with an almighty crash, and Hartley's momentum caused him to fall between the joists and land on top of it.

As Hartley had fallen forward, he had instinctively let go of the paraffin lamp, in order to break his fall. As he crashed down, the lamp had simultaneously landed on a section of floor boarding that had not been removed; it smashed, starting a small fire and sent a bead of flaming paraffin skittering across the room where it ignited the dry painters' dustsheets with an audible *whoof!*.

Below ground level, Hartley was initially unaware of the fire above him, so shocked was he at the bizarre sequence of events that led him to be lying there on the stone floor, knowing his friend was trapped in the subterranean chamber beneath him. He was momentarily paralysed with fear, as he could hear his friend's muffled screams. It was only then that he realised that a fire had started above him, but his first thought had to be for his friend. He tried to pull at the large ring in the middle of the slab – it was no good; he then grabbed the crow bar and thrust it between the two slabs in order to lever up the trap door. It creaked and scuffed but it was simply too heavy. He was almost weeping with desperation and panic; his heart pounded as the significance of his plight became ever clearer with each passing second. The heat on his upper body was now starting to intensify – he realised that he had to put out the fire before he could do anything else. He levered himself back up onto the floor above where he found a perilous situation:

The dry sheets had been matted with dust and paint from many a job over the years and had ignited instantly into a fireball; it, in turn, had licked the curtains that hung over the sheets and the timber trestles and planks that lay beside them. By the second, timbers and fabrics throughout the room were feeding the greedy flames. With denial his only ally, Hartley rushed into the adjacent room and ripped down the curtains in order to use them to beat the flames into submission. But in the few seconds he had been away, the fire had virtually consumed the room under where Carmichael was trapped – even the three exposed floor joists were now ablaze. Bill could barely get into the room as the flames appeared to be shoeing him away; futile beating only succeeded in causing the curtain itself to catch fire. As Hartley dropped the curtain, the flames leapt into the next room as if seeking out fresh prey.

With his face glistening with perspiration and soot, a sudden realisation struck Hartley that he had no chance of saving his friend. What should he do? *Get help! No! How do I explain? What about Tom? There's no time! Run! Run! RUN!*

He burst out of the front door and raced towards the Abbey Gate. A light came on in one of the houses to his right. He hesitated: *Is there time?* He glanced back – the whole of the ground floor was now ablaze – *NO! RUN! RUN!* He sprinted down Abbey Street and through the Irish Gate into Caldewgate, his legs racing as fast as his mind. Half way up the hill towards the Infirmary he finally stopped and looked back: he could already see a pillar of smoke rising into the windless air, like some great brooding genie from a bottle. Between him and the fire, lights were appearing and he imagined people in and around the Cathedral rushing out in panic as the beautiful house was being razed to the ground. He turned and ran.

Chapter Seventeen

Following His Namesake

Bill Hartley ran until he collapsed with exhaustion into a ditch, somewhere west of Kirkandrews on Eden. He must have been unconscious for several hours as, when he woke up, the sun was high. He sat up, still dazed, oblivious to the damp grass and muddy bed. Still in disbelief, as to the events of a few hours earlier, he set off again, with no intended destination in mind; but an almost subconscious instinct inevitably drew him back towards his home village.

Careful not to be seen by anyone on the road or upon his entry into Burgh, Hartley trudged into the large square cobbled yard to the rear of a row of cottages – one of which was his. He entered the shed where the horse was kept and slumped down onto the bench against the wall. Through stinging bloodshot eyes, he looked forlornly at the ground, still bewildered by the events of the last few hours. *What were we thinking of? Should I have stayed? If they managed to put the fire out, could Tom be saved?* He put his head in his hands and sobbed quietly.

The restless horse broke his trance and he looked up to see the animal tossing its head back, as if it were agitated by the mood of its master. Hartley's gaze fell on a length of rope that had been wound into a loop and hung on the wall above the horses head; he sat there, staring at the rope for several minutes. Quite deliberately, he got up and patted the horse's neck with one hand and reached for the rope with the other.

Oblivious to the time of day, and with his mind a complete blank, the carter left the yard in the dwindling light and headed for St Michael's Church; he entered the empty church unseen by anyone and made his way to the darkest nook, near the narrow entrance that led up to the bell tower.

After what seemed only a few minutes the latch of the church door clanked and a dark figure entered. Hartley instinctively backed into the dark alcove and put his shoulders against the stone wall behind him. The figure walked towards the front of the church and Hartley recognised Reverend Fraser who knelt down in one of the forward pews. Bill watched Fraser vacantly for some minutes before the restless vicar rose and started walking around the dimly-lit church.

He appeared to be looking for something as he finally walked across to the dark alcove where Hartley was hiding. Fraser peered into the murk – Hartley could see him but was himself completely protected from view by the shadows. Suddenly Richard seemed to start and spun round to see one of the candles on the altar go out. The Reverend appeared to conquer his curiosity at this point – he moved towards the door blowing out the remaining candles as he went. Finally, with the sound of the key turning in the lock, and a rattle of the door from the outside, he was gone.

Bill Hartley was now alone in the blackness of the church; he slid his back down the wall until he settled into a crouched position. There were no more tears – he was all cried out; there were no more thoughts – except one.

He waited what must have been a couple of hours – enough time for the Reverend and the rest of the village to settle quietly in for the night – before embarking on his final task. Leaving his hiding place, he began to drag his heavy legs up the stone stairs of the bell tower; the soles of his boots grating against the surface of the stone as he climbed. Finally reaching the timber platform of the bell tower – the rope he removed from the shed still looped over his shoulder – he stood looking at the bell, and listening to the light breeze as it eased through the apertures of the tower and gently wafted round the giant iron instrument.

Hartley took the rope from his shoulder and, grabbing one end, let the rest fall onto the platform with a splat. With some difficulty, he proceeded to fix the end of the rope to the mechanism above the bell, giving it several tugs to make sure it was secure. The tears returned as, quite deliberately, he picked up the other end of the rope and formed it into a noose which he placed round his neck, paying no regard to the six feet of slack that was still lying on the surface of the platform. He stood on the edge of the platform; the bell in front of him; the black abyss below.

Weeping audibly, the inner demons that had tormented his final hours were about to be silenced. He leapt off the edge, sending the rope on the timber platform into a frenzy until it became taught with a snapping jolt, and caused the giant bell to sound.

Chapter Eighteen

Laying Ghosts to Rest

"**A**lthough it probably never occurred to the poor chap at the time, it was a tragic case of history repeating itself." Cornelius Armstrong sat in the study of his friend Richard Fraser on the first Saturday afternoon in December 1907, almost two months since the double tragedy that had shaken the small village of Burgh by Sands.

Richard had invited the Carlisle detective to join him and some of the other villagers as they had arranged to gather for the first time since the tragedy and toast 'absent friends' in *The Lowther*, and try and bring some normality to the village in the process by starting the Christmas festivities. Upon meeting again, the two men had observed that it was almost exactly twelve months since the two had met at Henry Baker's Christmas Eve party. "Quite a twelve months!" said Richard thoughtfully, before asking Cornelius to take him through his deductions, over lunch.

The detective explained that when Hartley's body was lying in church and he smelled the smoke on his clothes, he suddenly realised what he and Carmichael had been up to. He requested the use of Fraser's telephone. His call was inevitably to Sergeant Townsend at the Police Station. His instruction: to get two men round to the scene of the fire in the Abbey and shovel out the ash from the sub-floor of the gutted house – "... I'll be there as soon as I can."

Inspector Armstrong arrived back at the Cathedral

grounds just in time to see PCs Green and Brady sweeping the last of the cinders away to reveal the large stone flags below.

"There!" he exclaimed jumping down onto the stone floor and pointing to a large iron ring that was set into a slab in the middle of what used to be one of the reception rooms. "This has been tampered with recently, see?" He pointed to the scuff marks between the joint the large flag and its neighbour – seemingly caused by a crowbar being wedged between the two and levered up. "Come on lads, let's get this up."

Armstrong removed his hat and coat and the three men went to work on lifting the heavy stone. They pulled on the iron ring and jammed a spade between the joint; this, and their brute force succeeded in pushing the thing upwards. After a great effort, they finally got it to the perpendicular and the three policemen leapt out of the way as it crashed back on itself, exposing the yawning black hole beneath it to daylight for the first time in centuries.

The Inspector and his men scrambled back to the edge and peered inside – there was no need for a lantern. The trap door had exposed a small chamber, about eight feet deep and six or seven paces square. Armstrong instantly recalled the similar cellar he had discovered under Blackfriars Street some months earlier. But it was the contents of the chamber that instantly grabbed the attention of the policemen.

"What the … ?" exclaimed Green over his superior's shoulder.

Directly under where the trap door had been, lay the body of a man in a grubby white shirt, black trousers and scuffed boots. His dreadful demise was etched on his distorted countenance: the blood appeared drawn from the man's face, turning it into an almost unrecognisable yellowish mask. But he was recognisable to Cornelius Armstrong.

"Who is it?" asked Brady.

"His name is Tom Carmichael," replied Armstrong. "It was him and his friend Bill Hartley who accidentally burned the house down. They were looking for treasure maps."

The two uniforms snorted simultaneously, "Treasure maps?" Green repeated, incredulous.

"It's a long story gentlemen," said Armstrong, "but once a man gets something in his head, it takes some shifting. Talking of shifting – let's get him out of there."

Armstrong and Green lowered themselves into the chamber and lifted Carmichael's body up through the hatch, where Brady dragged it out. PC Green quickly levered himself back out but Armstrong stopped as something caught his eye – there was something in the corner of the chamber. He squinted to allow his eyes to adjust to the shaded part of the underground compartment. "I don't believe it!" his voice echoed up through the hole in the ground.

"What is it sir," said one of his men.

"A skeleton," he declared. "Pass me down a lantern."

The skull was a green-white, in the pale beam of the lamp. Armstrong reached in his pocket for a handkerchief to hold over his nose and mouth, suddenly becoming aware of the vile stagnant air. The soft shaft of torchlight then picked something else up on the ground: a glint; a small disc? And another! Armstrong shone the torch around the floor and dusted some of the debris away with his foot. Coins were strewn all over the base of the chamber. He knew what this meant and looked again.

Beside the skeleton were the remains of a rotting wooden box; its corroded hinges and clasp hung precariously to what was left of the timber. Cornelius shone the lamp inside the box: there was nothing but dust and fragments of parchment. He picked up some fragments and rubbed them between his fingers and thumb, and smiled.

"It was Balliol's treasure maps," said Inspector Armstrong to Reverend Fraser, as he concluded his narrative.

"And the skeleton?" asked the vicar.

"I know Doctor Bell, the pathologist at the Infirmary," said Cornelius, "he once told me that he had an interest in anthropometrics, which apparently is the measurement of people. He examined what was left of the bones and suggested that they belonged to a man who was over six feet in height.

"I suggest, Richard, that the skeleton was that of Simon Ashbourne, the King's Courtier. Furthermore, I believe – as Hartley and Carmichael obviously did – that the contents of the box that he carried consisted of the bags of coins and, the far more valuable maps that detail the whereabouts of John Balliol's treasures."

Armstrong thought about the warning signs: his chance meeting with them in the Library back in May when they looked so shifty; the books in Carmichael's house detailing the history of the Cathedral and its derelict drainage system; their study group activity focusing on Balliol's maps; and finally the fire at the Abbey which was followed by Carmichael's disappearance and Hartley's suicide.

"It was only then that it all became perfectly clear in my mind. I am only sorry I never reasoned it sooner. I must say there is a part of me that admires the deduction work of Carmichael and Hartley. It's just a pity they couldn't couple that with a little more honesty."

Richard had been listening intently to the Inspector for over an hour when the chiming of the clock broke his reverie. "Good heavens!" he cried, "it is three o'clock. We had better go to the pub to meet the others. They will be wondering where we are."

The two men donned their outdoor wear once more and stepped out into the grey December afternoon. No sooner had Richard closed the gate to the vicarage behind him when he exclaimed, "I have forgotten my gloves! Do excuse me, Cornelius." He left the Inspector standing out on the pathway as he went back inside.

Cornelius idly waited for his friend in the fading afternoon light. His eye wandered this way and that until he suddenly jerked around to his right to see a tall, bearded man standing about fifty yards away on the edge of the marsh. He wore a long deep red cloak. The two men stood watching each other in an eerie silence, almost transfixed by the other's presence. Cornelius looked into the man's eyes and realised he was the

200

same figure he saw in the crowd at the six-hundred year celebrations on the marsh in July. Although his eyes were not as harsh and fiery as he had witnessed then, the man's stare still made the Inspector feel uncomfortable.

The Reverend suddenly slammed the door behind him, causing Armstrong to momentarily tear his gaze away from the man – when he looked back, he was gone.

"That's better!" said Fraser and then seeing Armstrong's face, "my dear fellow, what is it? You look as though you've seen a gh–"

"Don't say it!" interrupted Cornelius, with a raised hand. "I suggest we concentrate a little less on the fourteenth century and a little more on the twentieth. Let's just go and have that drink."

Historical Note

In the early twentieth century, Italian migrants were attracted to the area by the increase in population and with it, the ready market for confectionary, ice cream and fish and chips. It would appear that the immigrants blended into the city well and added to the diverse cultural mix which had been heavily influenced by their Celtic counterparts throughout the previous century.

There were very few instances of problems involving members of the Italian community, although in an early example of the 'ice cream wars' two Italians were charged in 1921 with having loaded guns in their ice cream vans!

There remains a sizable section of the city's population today who have Italian heritage and the city retains its fair share of Italian owned restaurants and fish and chip shops.

I am assuming that fish and chip shops – Italian or otherwise – were probably not uppermost in the thoughts of Henry III and Eleanor of Provence when the first child, the future Edward I, was born on 17th June 1239.

In adulthood, Edward was a tall man of six feet two inches (unusually tall for the time) and his long arms and legs earned him the nick-name, Longshanks. Edward was in the Holy Land when he heard of his father's death on 20th November 1272.

After spending much of his reign on crusades in the east, or on campaigns in France and Wales, Edward turned his attention to Scotland when his brother-in-law Alexander III, King of Scots died in 1286. He was asked to arbitrate by the Scottish Lords over who should become monarch. Edward chose John de Balliol, and this decision led to decades of Anglo-Scottish warfare.

Edward paid a number of visits to Carlisle during this period, using the city as his last English base before pursuing his military ambitions north of the Border. The scene of his meeting with Robert the Bruce in Carlisle Cathedral is based on a true event: Bruce initially pledged fealty to Edward before relations between the two deteriorated.

He was destined to make his final trip north in September 1306. The King was taken ill on the journey, and arrived at Lanercost Priory – eight miles east of Carlisle – on 29th September. Parliament had been summoned to meet in the city on 20th January 1307. The King was not well enough to attend and did not travel from Lanercost until 12th March. After a further fifteen weeks Edward finally left Carlisle on 26th June. Taken ill almost immediately, it took him almost a week to travel less than three miles to Kirkandrews-on-Eden. On 5th July he reached the small village of Burgh-by-Sands (which is pronounced bruff, not burgh) which lies near the mouth of the River Eden on the Solway Firth, around seven miles from Carlisle. Two days later on 7th July 1307 the King died on Burgh Marsh and his body was laid at the nearby church.

There is a red sandstone monument which rises from the marsh, and signifies the spot on which the King died.

Finally I must come clean and apologise for shattering any illusions my readers may have. Characters such as Rodger de Coventry, Simon Ashbourne and William Hartley are all fictitious and I'm afraid to report that there is no record of any hidden treasure or indeed of any ghost thought to be that of King Edward. They are all figments of my vivid (some would say twisted) imagination.

Martin Daley

The Casebook of Inspector Armstrong
Volume II

Detective Inspector Cornelius Armstrong will return soon in the second volume of his casebook. In *The Bells and Plate Fix*, Armstrong is troubled by the apparent accidental death of a man who falls a hundred feet from the Wetheral Viaduct. Cornelius puts his reputation on the line to disprove the verdict and in the process uncovers a corruption network of staggering proportions.

In the second short novel, *The Kaiser's Assassin*, Cornelius's holiday in the Lakes is interrupted when he is invited to Lowther Castle by the Earl of Lonsdale. His seemingly innocent visit ends in a race against time to foil a simmering plot to murder the visiting Wilhelm II.

For more information about books by Martin visit
www.martindaley.co.uk

"With five volumes you could fill that gap on that second shelf"
(Sherlock Holmes, *The Empty House*)

So why not collect all 44 murder mysteries from Baker Street Studios? Available from all good bookshops, or direct from the publisher with free UK postage & packing at just £7.50 each. Alternatively you can get full details of all our publications, including our range of audio books, and order on-line where you can also join our mailing list and see our latest special offers.

Baker Street Studios Limited, Endeavour House, 170 Woodland Road,
Sawston, Cambridge CB22 3DX
www.breesebooks.com, sales@breesebooks.com